M000165072

OPERATION AMBUSH

SUPER AGENT ROMANTIC SUSPENSE SERIES, BOOK 5

MISTY EVANS

Beach
Path
Publishing
LLC

Operation: Ambush, Super Agent Romantic Suspense Series, Book 5

Copyright ©2020 by Misty Evans

ISBN: 978-1-948686-24-2

Print: 978-1-948686-25-9

Cover Art by Fanderclai Design

Formatting by Beach Path Publishing, LLC

Editing by Patricia Essex

To Mark—pour toujours et toujours.

To love someone deeply gives you strength. Being loved by someone deeply gives you courage.
—Lao Tzu

ONE

In the past two months, CIA operative John Quick had ridden a camel through the rough terrain of Afghanistan, set off a bomb under the Kremlin in Moscow, and spent time under-cover inside a Mexican prison. The bomb had been fun, right up his alley. The rest, not so much.

Still, it was what he did. He put his life on the line for his country every day. He lived and breathed this shit, and never doubted himself or his mission. Ever.

Standing in front of the Morgan family retreat in upstate New York, none of his recent special ops missions compared to the personal nightmare he was about to embark on. Doubts made him sweat, and he wiped some from his forehead. His feet involuntarily shifted and he leaned one hand on the door in front of him to steady himself for a moment.

What the ever-livin' hell was *that* about?

Get it together, man. Don't lose your balls now.

His finger hovered over the doorbell. The Morgan vacation home—one of six mansions owned by the billionaire financier, Charles Morgan—was more than your average cabin in the woods. From the intel John had gathered—and he never went into enemy territory without knowing the layout—the multi-story log and glass home situated on Otsego Lake boasted five bedrooms, an equal amount of bathrooms, a theater, a wine cellar, and a complete spa. The six acres surrounding it contained a boat dock, tennis courts, a pool, and a zip line in the woods behind the house.

Who the hell lived like this?

The cabin, like all the mansions, was the type of place Lucie Morgan—the woman of his dreams—belonged in. Not his simple, unadorned one-bedroom apartment in D.C.

She's so far out of my reach, I shouldn't even be standing here.

Conversation and laughter filtered through the window nearby. Soft music, the clink of glasses and silverware. The sounds of family and friends.

What was he doing here? This was no place for a man with no family, no home, no life outside his job.

You're on vacation.

Vacation. That's what Conrad Flynn, the spook in charge of Pegasus called it, but it was basically forced leave. Normal people liked time off. They looked forward to it. Sleeping in, hitting the beach, spending time away from their jobs.

Normal people went to fucking Disneyland. Or on a cruise to Alaska. The Bahamas.

While he wasn't actually a spook for the CIA, like the infamous Flynn, he wasn't exactly your average, "normal", Joe, either. While he'd never set foot inside Disneyland, he'd once done a search and rescue in the Bahamas and always thought he might go back someday. An ex–military operative with the highly trained and efficient Team Pegasus, he rescued lost spies, hunted down various folks trapped in foreign prisons, and acted as a bodyguard in third-world countries when certain covert deals were going down. Like all the men in Pegasus, he was on call 24/7.

Until now.

Vacation or not, he didn't belong here. He was adding fuel to the fire of his relationship with Lucie. His *non*-relationship with Lucie. Rehabbing an old house into a dance studio and spending a few nights together here and there was not a relationship, though Lucie wanted it to be. She'd made that clear. He'd tried squashing that crazy idea any time it came up, but here he was, because he just couldn't stay away from her.

She was his drug of choice. The way she smelled like lilacs. Her heavy and extremely sexy French accent. The way her big sky-blue eyes were always searching his, as if he held all the answers to life, or the Universe, or some such shit. The way her lips felt when she kissed him, the way they teased him when she laughed.

Everything about her sent him searching for those answers she wanted. Whatever her desire was, he wanted to give it to her.

Him. A guy with nothing to offer but himself. And that wasn't much, no matter how you looked at it.

He lowered his finger from the doorbell and cast a glance over his shoulder. On the sweeping driveway, his four-wheel-drive truck, rusty and ugly in the midst of BMWs and Mercedes, stood positioned for a quick getaway. It wasn't too late to turn around. Not too late to text Lucie and claim he'd been called away on a job—

His phone rang.

Maybe it won't be a lie.

Caller ID read "Boy Scout".

Lawson Vaughn, his boss. One of them, anyway.

Busted.

He debated hitting the button. What were the odds

Lawson was actually calling about a mission? "Hey, man. I was just going to text you. Flynn's worried about one of his spies stuck in Syria. I'm heading to D.C. in case Pegasus needs to perform an extraction. The team and I—"

"Aren't going anywhere," the Pegasus leader said. "Get your ass in here with that six-pack, Johnnie boy, or I'm coming out to get you. That's an order."

John instinctively looked up. Lawson stood in front of a floor-to-ceiling window on the second floor. Inside enemy territory.

Lawson, Lucie's soon-to-be brother-in-law, waved. He was about to take the plunge and marry Lucie's sister. He was one brave—or maybe sick—man.

Setting down the beer, John waved back with a single finger. His favorite one, right in the middle. He moved away from the door a few steps and lowered his voice. "I can't do this."

"Bullshit. You can handle a simple party."

"A party with a bunch of strangers who mean nothing to me? Nothing I love better." He'd slapped a red bow on a six-pack of Bud as a gift to the expecting parents. They were going to need a whole case when the kid was born. "A party with Lucie's highfalutin' family? Send me back to Afghanistan, man. Shit, even another goddamn Mexican prison would be a fucking *picnic* compared to this."

"Suck it up."

How many times had they demanded that of each other in the past five years since John had taken over as Lawson's operations captain? "This isn't even a *party* party. It's a freakin' baby shower." He was so out of his element here, even his fingernails were sweating. "Family, babies...kill me now. Nothing I did with the Berets prepared me for this. I'm getting hives thinking about it."

"You want to see Lucie, don't you?"

Did soldiers love guns? He turned back and looked up again. "Awww, hell, Law." His Texas drawl, rising with his panic, turned one-syllable words into multi-syllables. "You know I do, but this is—"

"Normal. Family get-togethers and baby showers are *normal*. You should try it."

In Lawson's world, this *was* normal. In John's? "Sucks to be you."

A lie. John envied Lawson's upcoming nuptials and impending fatherhood, but no way could he see himself in Lawson's shoes. He'd seen other operatives lose their edge, worrying too much about those they'd left behind. He wasn't about to second-guess every decision in the field because he didn't want to leave a wife without a husband or kids without a dad.

So even though he'd wanted that elusive *something more* with Lucie since he'd rescued her from a terrorist the previous year—*what a way to meet*—it wasn't going to happen. She unraveled him...screwed with his brain, his emotions, his...everything.

He couldn't—no, he *wouldn't*—settle down. Not for her. Not for anyone. Whatever fantasy she was cooking up about them enjoying a future like Lawson and her sister, Zara, was just that—a fantasy.

No matter how much he wished it could be reality.

Then Lawson, the Yankee ballbuster who acted as honorably as a Boy Scout, said the one phrase John couldn't walk away from. "Do it for me."

Low blow. John turned his back on the door, on Lawson.

He scanned the frozen lake lined with snow-covered trees.

Picture postcard and all that shit. Stalling, he tried to think of something witty to say. "Who knew Flynn would allow one of his super agents like Zara to get pregnant?"

"Believe it or not, Director Flynn cannot control everything."

Dark gray clouds hung low in the distance. Another Canadian front swinging in. That could work to his advantage. A few minutes of face time at the party where he could drool over Lucie and log some mental pictures for future fantasizing, and then he could use the approaching storm as an excuse to cut and run. In and out in under an hour.

Disneyland was nice this time of year, right? Warm weather, Mickey Mouse, and not a Morgan family baby shower in sight.

Bailing on Lucie, after all she's been through, would be a shit-ass thing to do.

Not to mention disappointing Lawson, his best friend. Good thing John was an ace at disappointing people.

"Is that the best you could find to wear?" Lawson's voice held a slight air of exasperation.

Lowering his head, John looked down at the tips of his worn-out cowboy boots. Snow clung to the edges of his olive drab BDUs. Though he was no longer Army, he still wore the pants with T-shirts and flannels. They were as much a part of him as his social awkwardness around Lucie.

Maybe today she'd finally see him the way he really was. He didn't belong in her world, and he wasn't about to change in order to fit in with the Morgan family, no way in hell.

"I came straight from Dulles. No time to run home and put on my fancy clothes"—never mind that he only owned a total of one dress shirt and a single pair of black slacks—"but, hey, if I'm not dressed good enough for you and the future in-laws..."

Lawson issued a heavy sigh. "Speaking of in-laws, the

sharks are circling in here. Lucie's sinking fast. She needs you, John."

The call to duty. *She needs you.*

Goddammit. Of all the people and relationships he'd walked away from in his life, he couldn't walk away from someone who needed him.

And Lawson—*damn him*—knew it.

Facing the door again, John glanced up at his boss. The man he followed into the fire on a regular basis. The man who'd saved his ass more than once.

John owed him. He owed Lucie, too. "You better not be fucking with me, Boy Scout."

Three fingers rose in the air.

John shook his head, snorted. But something brewed deep in his gut. If the Morgans were giving Lucie a hard time, he'd clean the deck with them.

For kicks, he gave Lawson the Star Trek Vulcan salute. *"De Oppresso Liber,* man." *To Free the Oppressed,* the Beret motto. "I'm coming in."

Before he lost his nerve, he pocketed the phone and raised his mental shields—he had issues about his own dysfunctional family he needed to keep suppressed. Up went his impassive poker face, the one he preferred for awkward social events, as he snatched his gift from the spot on the deck.

He raised his finger to ring the doorbell.

Put it back down.

Fuck the doorbell. Guerrilla warfare worked best when you took the enemy by surprise.

TWO

John Quick was smokin' hot.

So hot, in fact, Lucie nearly dropped the tray of punch-filled champagne glasses when he entered the great room without even knocking.

Lucie's sister, Zara, all big belly and goofy smile, sat forward on the sofa and yelled, "John! You made it."

A fire crackled in the large stone fireplace. Her father and Agent Saunders, the FBI agent who'd been so kind to Lucie and her sister after their ordeal with the terrorist, Alexandrov Dmitri, last year, stood in front of the fireplace discussing stock options and gold futures.

Zara's mother sat on the sofa next to her daughter, the two of them surrounded by aunts, nieces, and cousins talking about strollers and how soon to apply for private schools.

Lucie, kept at arm's length all day by everyone but Zara, had been passing out the nonalcoholic punch and holding back an eye roll. The baby wasn't even born yet and the Morgan clan was in an uproar over which private school the kid would attend. Agent Saunders, sensing Lucie's exasperation, had winked at her and grinned. He was good like that...making her feel at ease in uncomfortable situations. He'd rescued her from plenty of those after the kidnapping when she'd had to recount what happened over and over to various government agencies.

A good guy, just like John...the man she daydreamed about on an hourly basis now standing in the entryway, trailing in snow and staring straight at her.

Some of the women giggled behind their hands. Her father's face fell. Regardless that John was a hero, her father didn't like him. On the two occasions the men had interacted, John had refused to talk about his family, his education, or his job history—the very cornerstones of the Morgan family. Everything her father held dear. From that point on, her brilliant, if snobbish father, had made no secret that he thought John was using Lucie to get to the Morgan money.

It had unfortunately happened before.

John didn't seem to care what anyone thought. He wore camouflage pants, a knit hat with a hole in it, and cowboy boots. His jaw was covered with a couple days' worth of stubble, his long hair peeked out from the hat, and he was carrying a six-pack of beer with a red bow on it.

Framed by the open door and surrounded by the rugged backdrop and falling snow, John looked completely at home. Except maybe for the scowl on his face. The tiniest bit of panic in his eyes.

For a long moment, Lucie simply stood and soaked him in.

"Hey," he said.

"Lawson!" Zara yelled at the top of her lungs. "John's here."

Behind Lucie, their father cleared his throat. Morgans did not yell.

While he'd fathered them both, Charles Morgan had never married Lucie's mother, and Zara was the only Morgan who treated Lucie as blood relation. So while the head of the

Morgan clan and his "legitimate" family claimed to accept Lucie as one of them, they hadn't *really* accepted anything other than the fact Lucie was getting a big fat trust fund payout on Monday when she turned thirty. Few seemed happy about that.

Like turning thirty wasn't daunting enough.

Zara struggled to get her pregnant self to her feet to greet John, and Lucie hastily set the tray on the large glass coffee table. As she grabbed one of her sister's hands, John strode across the wood floor, dropping snow as he went, and gently took Zara's other. Together, the two of them helped her stand.

Zara, always amenable and outgoing, had become even more so during her pregnancy. Hormones, Lawson claimed. She threw her arms around John and hugged him hard. "We're so glad you came."

Lucie felt a spurt of jealousy. Not because Zara and John had become friends, but because her sister had no reservations when it came to saying and showing what she felt. Not even in front of the stuffy, no-public-displays-of-emotion family they belonged to.

John wasn't a PDA type of guy either, but he accepted the hug with grace. Over Zara's shoulder, he met Lucie's stare with his brilliant blue eyes and an embarrassed smile raising the corners of his lips. "Lucie invited me. How could I say no?"

The sound of his deep voice with its slight Texas drawl, combined with that look, sent Lucie's pulse into the red zone and her mind into the past. It had been nearly two months...

Two long, agonizing months since the last time his full lips had teased her mouth into submission. Two months since that lazy drawl had laced his voice when he'd murmured in her ear, "I can't wait to get that sweet little body of yours under me."

She shivered. Yep, John Quick was hot.

A hot, sexy hero who'd saved her the previous year from

Dmitri, and still invaded her dreams on a daily basis. With his long, lean frame, blue eyes, and sly smile, he regularly took center stage in her daydreams, her night dreams, and every spare second she wasn't trying to fit into the Morgan family's way of life.

There were dreams of him in nothing but his cowboy boots pounding her against the bedroom wall. Dreams of his strong arms holding her up as they had sweaty sex in the back of his truck. In the shower. On the kitchen table—

Another throat-clearing interrupted her lascivious thoughts. She blushed and John smiled for real. Did he know what she'd been thinking? Of course, he did. He was no doubt thinking similar ones about her.

Plastering on her practiced Morgan face, she took his hand as he broke away from Zara's embrace. "Everyone, this is John Quick, the man who rescued me last year. John, this is my family."

Sort of.

John tensed and Lucie wondered if she'd said something wrong. Having grown up in France with a French mother, she often mixed up her words in English. Not as much now as when she'd first moved to America, but sometimes she didn't understand the subtleties of the culture or slang. Every once in a while, she said the wrong thing, implied the wrong meaning.

To the Morgan clan, it was another reason to dismiss her, and one of the reasons she stayed quiet around them. Once she got her trust fund, they'd realize she didn't care about the money. She intended to give most of it away and the rest she would use to help the kids at the ballet studio. What she wanted was a family.

Zara, coming to her rescue, patted John's arm. "He and Lawson are both heroes, but they hate hearing it."

Her father stepped forward, hand outstretched, even though he looked like he'd rather shake a rat's tail. "John."

No "good to see you" or "glad you could make it." Just the briefest acknowledgment that sounded like a warning.

Agent Saunders also shook John's hand. "It's been a while. I hear Flynn's keeping you guys busy."

"Good to see you again, Matt," he replied, his casual body stance and soft tone covering up that panic she'd seen in his gaze.

Another tiny spurt of jealousy flared in her stomach. Agent Saunders probably knew more about John than she did, since they'd worked together. "Agent Saunders was in New York for a meeting and was available to drive out to join us."

The man smiled at her. "Kind of you to invite me, Lucie. It's good to see you and Zara, and your family, under enjoyable circumstances. The party is a nice getaway for me, and I'm glad I could make it."

At that moment, Zara's own hero entered the room. Lawson and John embraced, slapping each other on the back. "About time you arrived, Johnnie boy. I was starting to think you'd chickened out."

John smiled but it resembled more of a sneer. "Wouldn't miss it for the world, man."

Liar. He and Lawson exchanged some kind of nonverbal message and Lucie bit the inside of her bottom lip. This exchange was for show, some kind of inside joke they so often seemed to share.

John didn't want to be here.

I should have known he wouldn't.

But she'd needed him. Needed to talk to him. He was so committed to Pegasus, their relationship had never had a chance to develop more fully. John had told her he didn't like commitments, that they were doomed before they started because of his job, and yet, it was the only thing she thought about these days. A relationship. With a man who didn't care who she was or what her last name was. A relationship with John.

And that's why she'd invited him.

That and the sex dreams.

Getting him to the cabin wasn't just about Zara and Lawson's baby. Or having John meet her family. If things went her way, Lucie was going to kidnap him for the weekend.

She had everything planned, right down to making Lawson swear on a bible that John wouldn't get called in for a mission. Although John had insisted he didn't want a relationship, Lawson had told her he was just scared.

Well, she was scared, too. Relationships were difficult and painful and sometimes even self-destructive. But they could be healthy and fun as well. Good things, including friendships and closer ties to family, could come out of tragic events and unfortunate past circumstances. Like the kidnapping. Because of that horrible event, she and Zara had a stronger bond than ever. They were sisters, sure, but they were also the best of friends.

All she had to do was persuade John that not only could he have a loving, long-term relationship, but that he *deserved* one. That would be the tricky part. She herself sometimes struggled with doubts about her worth, as a person, not a Morgan heir. While John didn't have a billionaire father people cowed to—in fact, just the opposite—he lacked perspective about his value in this world just as much as she did.

Reaching for the beer gift, she let her fingers linger over his as they touched. "We should put that in the fridge, yes?"

He let her take the six-pack and shrugged off his coat. Grabbing Lucie by the hand, he leaned in and gave her fingers a slight squeeze. "*Oui*," he answered in her native tongue, all traces of his Texas accent disappearing.

His gaze rambled over her dress, down to her shoes. "Let's put them on some ice."

Her pulse jumped. *Ice.* Good idea. The things he could do to her with an ice cube...

Ice cube...kitchen...kitchen table.

Oh, yeah, the kitchen table was definitely on her list of fantasies to act out this weekend. As was the hot tub, and the shower, and...

John tilted his head slightly, as if he were reading her carnal thoughts.

Keeping a straight face, she tugged him toward the kitchen at the back of the cabin. "You can help me with the cake."

Cake. Frosting. *John lying on the kitchen table with frosting all over his body...*

Blushing, Lucie put her head down as she walked past her father, unable to keep the grin off her face.

God. Why was she so nervous? Zara and Lawson had primed her for this weekend, but now as she led him into the expansive chef's kitchen, where they could be alone, she felt like an actor with stage fright.

Removing a bottle of beer from the carton, she toyed with it before placing it in the giant stainless steel refrigerator, already overflowing with food and drink. "You never told me you speak French."

John leaned on the center island, his gaze taking in the Viking appliances, marble countertops, and catered food covering every surface. "I can't. I'm only fluent in terrorist-speak, Vulcan signs, and hostage negotiations."

She'd witnessed two out of three of those firsthand. She still had nightmares where John and Lawson didn't show up at Dmitri's compound in time, and she and Zara died. "You didn't like it when I introduced you to the family."

He met her eyes, crossed his arms over his chest. "It wasn't that. My job is classified. I don't tell people what I do for a living."

Way to go, Luce. She should have thought of that.

"*J'ai fait une gaffe.*" She looked away and slid another bottle onto the shelf. "I made a mistake."

Reaching for a shrimp cup, he shrugged. "Your family already knows about Zara's undercover work, and Law's job with Pegasus. They had to in the aftermath of the kidnapping. Guess it's not a big deal."

But it was. She could tell. Outside the large window above the kitchen sink, she caught sight of a red truck. "Did you drive all the way here from D.C.?"

Another shrug. "I have some time off. Driving clears my head."

Lawson had told her John was on a forced vacation after getting in that morning from his latest mission. She didn't understand why anyone would have to be forced to take time off work, but apparently, his last two missions had gone badly and John was unhappy. Stressed out. *Making poor decisions,* Lawson had said. He needed time out of the field.

A perfect reason to kidnap him and keep him at the cabin all weekend. She had several stress-reducers in mind.

Had he thought about her at all when he was away?

"I'm staying here for the weekend." She placed the last bottles of beer into the fridge and shut the door before leaning against it. "You could stay with me. Clear your head here."

The casual air he'd been projecting disappeared even though nothing about his body changed. He studied her, those blue eyes intense. Penetrating. "Crowded in with the rest of the family?"

"They're leaving." Soon, too, by the way they'd been acting. Fine with her. Now that John was here, she would happily ship them all out. "It would be only you and me."

The penetrating stare turned warm. Not warm, *hot.*

Look out, kitchen table.

She was sure he was going to say yes. Then he crossed his arms again. "I'm on call for Pegasus. I should get back to D.C."

Lawson had warned her John would do this. Resist.

"Bullshit," she said and saw the surprise on John's face.

Thing was, Lucie knew what she wanted. So many things became clear after seeing the inside of a terrorist compound. After being drugged and used as bait. After nearly losing your one and only sister, and nearly dying alongside her.

You never knew when some terrorist was going to come along and screw up your life. All the plans she'd had for the future had taken on new meaning. Living for today became more important.

As the French would say, she needed to *bite life with full teeth.*

Which was why she was trying so hard with her American family. Her mother back in Paris had recently given Lucie her blessing to reach out to Charles and move to Arlington to be near Zara. After her ordeal with Dmitri, Lucie longed to be part of this family more than anything in the world. To belong with them. Share her secrets with them. Forge new relationships.

So far, she had the last name and a trust fund. She was still working on the belonging part.

John's lips pressed into a tight line. He didn't like being called on his lie.

The only other thing Lucie wanted was John. "It's my birthday." And he would be her present. *If* she pulled this off. "On Monday."

His brows went up and he looked chagrined. "Why didn't you tell me? I would have gotten you something."

Time to take that bite out of life.

Pushing away from the fridge, she gave him a return look she hoped conveyed what she was planning as she walked over and planted her Louboutins in front of him. Forcing his arms to uncross, she wrapped them around her waist, pressing her breasts and hips against him. "All I want is you. For the weekend."

His body, so tense it practically vibrated, shifted to accommodate her. The hot look returned to his eyes. He rested his hands on her hips and searched her face. For what, she wasn't sure.

Glancing at her lips, he lowered his voice. "Lucie, I—"

"Please." She touched his chin, ran her fingers over the stubble there. "Stay with me tonight. One night. That is all I ask. You don't have to make promises."

There was sex in those blue eyes when they met hers again. He wanted her as badly as she wanted him. The chemistry between them had been there since their first meeting, when she'd looked like hell and he'd looked like the action hero he was, saving her from guns and bullets and a madman with a biological weapon. The one thing he couldn't save her from was her heart.

John was a workaholic. Everyone in America was. Even her father, who was rich enough to retire ten times over. He never stopped talking business, and John never stopped leaving on missions.

Lately, she wondered if he was actually saving people and taking out terrorists, or was he running from her?

She almost said "please" again, but held her tongue.

When she and Zara had discussed her "kidnapping" plan, it had seemed so easy. Lucie had felt energized, alive, and Zara had told her to be direct and assertive. That's what guys like Lawson and John needed, she'd said. A woman who could hold her own and tell them what she wanted.

In twenty-nine years and three hundred and sixty-three days, Lucie had never had trouble telling a man what she wanted. But John was different.

"I want..." She took a deep breath, forced her gaze to stay on his. "I want you."

There. Simple. Direct. Assertive.

Something flashed in his eyes. Surprise?

More like regret.

Was he going to tell her no? Reject her?

Rejection. A familiar shadow these days. Her heart broke into a thousand tiny grains of sand. She took half a step back.

John grabbed her by the arms. "Where you goin', darlin'?"

Darlin'. The drawl sent shivers up and down her spine. "The cake. I need to cut the cake and plate it."

"The cake can wait." He lowered his lips to hers. "I can't."

The kiss was as hot as the man. He crushed her lips, drew back, and licked her bottom one. Crushed them again. His tongue pushed its way in—as if she would resist—and *bam*. His hands were all over her. Grabbing her ass, running up and down her spine, cupping her breasts.

Lucie's hands weren't exactly still. Fire ignited under her skin, and she tore off his hat, raking her hands through his long hair. Tugging on it. Clutching at his shoulders to bring him closer.

In the other room, the music continued to play. Zara laughed.

John spun them both around, grabbed her by the ass cheeks, and lifted her onto the island's countertop. A tray of mini quiches went flying.

"What the..." he said, drawing his hand away and examining his finger.

Lucie's pulse beat a staccato in her ears. "What is it?"

"Nothing. Just a scratch, but something back here..." He

peered over her shoulder, held up the silver cake server. "Are
you cutting cake with this or severing a limb?"

Don't get distracted. Lucie took the cake server with its
serrated edge and tossed it over to the kitchen sink. *Be direct.
Assertive.*

Let me kiss it and make it better. She'd heard American
women say that to their kids. The skin wasn't broken, and she
met his eyes with a half-lidded look, drew his finger to her
mouth, and wrapped her lips around it. Slow and seductive, she
slid her tongue over the tip and down. Back up.

A French kiss to make it better. He shuddered. Tightening
her lips, she sucked. Hard.

His body jerked. Pushing between her legs, he sent his
rough hands under the hem of her dress, sliding it up her thighs
with his free hand before he spread her legs wide.

She released his finger and clung to him. He was hard and
she was soft, and she opened for him, cradling him and wanting
more. He moaned softly into her mouth as he kissed her again,
and she wrapped her legs around him.

The real thing, even with her clothes on and her family in
the next room, was even hotter than in her dreams.

Embracing his strong shoulders, she hung on as the room
spun. Tongue to tongue with him, her breasts smashed against
his rock-hard chest, his erection pressed into the spot between
her legs.

The only barrier between them was the clothing. Flimsy
stuff, that. Lucie gripped the lapels of John's flannel shirt and
gave them a yank.

Buttons flew. His chest emerged. All that luscious skin, a
tattoo over his left pec. Those rippling muscles.

In the background, someone cleared his throat. Loudly.
"What in God's name is going on in here?"

THREE

JOHN JERKED BACK, breaking the kiss and sucking in a breath. He spun, saw Charles's attention drop to his very out-there erection—thank God he still had on his pants— and spun back.

"Um..." Words evaded him. His brain was trapped in his zipper. When was the last time he'd been caught making out with a hot girl by her dad? Hell, when was the last time he'd lost control like that? "We were just, um, getting ready to cut the cake."

Somehow that came out wrong, at least to John's ears. Agitated, he looked at Lucie just in time to see a sly grin cross her lips. Lips that were swollen from his kisses. She tried to re-button his shirt. There were only two buttons left.

"I see." Out of the corner of his eye, John saw Charles looking at the floor and the scattering of food. "What was that crash?"

He knew damn well what the crash was. Bastard wanted to put them further on the hooks. See if he could draw blood.

Sharks always did. They thought they were better than everyone else, even their own flesh and blood.

Anger simmered in John's gut. He'd been swimming with sharks his whole life. One thing he knew: sharks could bleed, too.

But this was Lucie's dad. He had to play it cool. "An accident, sir. I slipped and dropped a tray."

"Lucie?" Charles asked.

She popped her head up over John's shoulder, the grin smothered. "*Oui?*"

"Are you all right?"

"Fine, Father."

"Then get down from there and clean up this mess."

Her body deflated. She looked down, eyelashes dark against her pale skin, and nodded. "I'll get a broom."

John backed away and helped her off the island, hating it when she pulled down the knit dress to cover her gorgeous legs. Hating the way all the life went out of her at her dad's orders.

Get a broom? What was she, the Morgans' personal maid? John covertly straightened his pants. "I'll get the broom. Tell me where it is."

She laid a hand on his arm. "I'll take care of it."

She disappeared through a side door. John, erection now gone, faced Charles. *The sharks are circling...* "Nice party. Lucie's amazing, isn't she? Doing all this for Z and Lawson? You must be very proud of her."

Charles narrowed his eyes. "Have you been drinking, son?"

Son. The word stuck in his craw. Nobody had the right to call him that. Never had.

It would have been easy to put the shark in his place. Make him regret he'd ever said it. Easy, but not smart. He wanted to like the guy, for Lucie's sake. At the very least, get along with him. "No, sir."

The two of them glared at each other across the kitchen tiles. Charles's attention traveled from John's mussed hair down to his boots. His face said he found John lacking in every area. "Perhaps it's time you left, Mr. Quick."

Not on your life. How ironic. He hadn't wanted to be here, and now no one was going to force him to leave.

John leaned against the island and crossed his feet at the ankles, making himself comfortable. "Think I'll stick around. I have a thing for cake." *And your daughter. Whom you don't appreciate, but I do.*

Charles stood his ground. "I know why you're here. What you're up to."

Seemed obvious after the island ordeal. "And?"

"You'll never get your hands on my money."

Wait. *What?* John scoffed. "I assure you I have no interest in your money."

Another scathing inventory of his hair, clothes, and boots. "Every man who has dated a female member of my family has been after the Morgan money. Lucie's trust fund could set you up for life, but believe me, I know how to deal with leeches like you."

The anger threatened to break free. "I don't know anything about a goddamn trust fund, and rest assured, neither Lawson nor I care about your Richey Rich pot of money. Maybe you should stop judging everyone by your standards, since money seems to be more important to you than your own family."

Charles's jaw worked, an angry flush coloring his cheeks. "Careful, son. You don't know me or my family, but I know all about men like you. Playing on a young woman's vulnerability. Convincing her you love her."

I do love—

Whoa. The shark needed a reality check and so did he. "Lucie and I are...friends." They were more than that, obviously, but what exactly *were* they? "Good friends fixin' to spend the weekend together."

Charles's brows rose and he stuttered for a moment, then cleared his throat. His eyes went steely. "You expect me to believe your intentions are proper?"

Proper? Yeah, right. "I don't care what you believe, Mr. Morgan, but my intentions are to treat Lucie the way she deserves to be treated. You might do the same."

Broom and dustpan in hand, Lucie returned and stopped. Just froze, scanning both their faces. She knew trouble when she saw it, and she pasted on a fake smile. "Everything okay?"

The tension in the room was as thick as the frosting on the cake. John took the broom and dustpan from her and started sweeping. "Your pop was saying what an amazing party this was, weren't you, Mr. Morgan?"

The man harrumphed and opened his mouth to respond when his cell phone rang. Setting his jaw, he gave John the stink eye and turned on his heel, answering the phone with a terse, "Morgan."

As he left through the side door, Lucie gave John a worried glance. "What happened?"

He made work of cleaning up the kitchen floor. "Just bonding with your ol' man."

She was silent for a long minute. So long, he almost dropped the broom and resumed their make-out session. Anything to get her to stop worrying about gaining her father's approval.

John knew from experience that hanging out in your head only led to regret. Guilt. Embarrassment.

Way to go, John. He may not have cared about family, but like Lawson and Zara, Lucie did.

And now, here he was dropping to hands and knees to scoop up the last of the crumbs on the kitchen floor, wishing all the messes he made in life were as easy to clean up.

Two pink shoes came into view, planting themselves in his

way. He didn't look up, just sat back on his haunches. "Look, Luce. I'm sorry. I shouldn't have—"

"The sooner we feed them cake," she interrupted, "the sooner they'll leave."

Taking his time, he did a slow perusal from her feet up her shapely calves, then higher, soaking her in just the way he'd planned. He had to touch her thighs, so he did, running his hands up under her dress. Lucie's chest heaved in and out. She swallowed hard.

Her cheeks were still flushed. Her hair as mussed as his. He stood, set the broom aside. "Cake it is."

She went for the cake server, washing it off in the sink.

He grabbed the plates.

The sharks were circling, but not for much longer. No one —not even the billionaire who owned the place—was going to make John leave Lucie's side.

SHE'D CALLED IT—LAWSON and Zara were still eating cake when the other Morgans began packing up and drifting out the door, parting with air kisses and promises of future get-togethers. Agent Saunders was long gone, saying he wanted to beat the incoming weather, but not before he'd taken a minute to thank Lucie for inviting him, holding her hand and complimenting her on the food and decorations. Lucie had beamed and John had felt a spurt of pride.

Snow fell in earnest as Zara's mother, Olivia, stood at the door, wrapped in a white fur and tapping an impatient foot. "Where is he?"

"I don't know," Zara said. Lawson had taken some plates to the kitchen, so she looked at John with pleading eyes. "Would you see if you can find my father?"

Gaining the Morgans' trust was John's first step in building an insurgency inside enemy territory. The ol' man might be a bust today, but his wife might be easier to win over. "I'll be happy to look for him."

"Thank you," she said, and Olivia offered him a reserved smile.

In the past twenty minutes, Charles had been on his cell phone constantly, disappearing into the bowels of the house every time it rang, and looking disgruntled when he came back. When he did rejoin them, all he did was complain about the cell service. How the whole world wanted a piece of him and his money.

When he'd said that, he'd looked at John.

John acted oblivious. Let him think whatever he wanted. Meanwhile, every time Charles left the room, John went to work infiltrating the rest of the clan. While surreptitiously holding his shirt together, he befriended Charles's brother, chatted with Zara's mother, and had several of Lucie's cousins laughing at his jokes, all in short order. He made sure his good ol' boy charm was hard to resist. Anything to piss off Charles Morgan.

Now, he headed in the direction Charles had last disappeared earlier. The living room, dining room, and a library were lumped into one great room. Beyond that, he didn't know what he'd find. Stairs to the second floor, it turned out. A bathroom and a hallway that led to the back of the house where an indoor pool overlooked the woods. Back to the hall and around the corner and he was next to the kitchen.

This house was a damn maze.

During the time Charles had been on the phone, John had identified several Morgans who were not happy with the man. Mostly they were pissed that Charles was giving Lucie money —not hard to figure that out—but underneath the surface, their discontent ran deeper. Some recent investments he'd recommended had gone south. They'd lost money.

Too bad he didn't have time to get the details, and maybe it was no big deal. Everyone got disgruntled when money was on the line. Sure, Charles acted like an ass every time John was around, and some of the distant relatives at the party confirmed he was a taciturn and somewhat eccentric billionaire, but he was also a self-starter. A man to admire. He'd built an entire empire in his lifetime. Done some good things with his money. Probably done some shitty ones, too.

From John's perspective, he was all hat and no cattle. It all came easy to Charles Morgan. Too easy.

And from the sound of it, Lucie's father seemed to think he had to make it hard for everyone else. Especially Lucie. It wasn't any of John's business, but he couldn't stand the way Charles treated her like a second-class citizen. He didn't understand why she put up with it.

Midway down the hall, John heard a man's voice, urgent and aggravated behind a wooden door.

Definitely Charles. He started to knock, caught part of Charles's words, and stilled.

"Why won't you leave me alone? I told you, I had nothing to do with that. Your mother made her choices, and..."

His voice trailed off as if listening to the person on the other end. "No. I will not be threatened. You come near me or my family again, and I'll go to the police."

Whoa. Charles was being threatened? By whom?

He should ask. Help the guy out. But billionaires received threats every day, didn't they? Didn't they have people to handle that?

Your mother made her choices.

John lowered his fist. Did Charles have another secret kid running around?

The pain it had caused Lucie made John cringe. Lucie and Zara would have accepted another member of this dysfunctional family without pause. The rest of the Morgans? Not so much.

Whatever. Family dramas didn't interest him. He just wanted the man out of the cabin. He had business to take care of with a certain beautiful woman.

Bam, bam, bam. The wooden door was solid as a rock under his fist. "Hey, Chuck. Your wife's looking for you."

Silence, and then a few seconds later, the door flew open. The man stood there, red-faced and practically blowing steam out his ears. The phone was clutched in his hand, an office with expensive furniture and heavy drapes behind him. "Don't you ever call me that again."

John couldn't help but smile at the veiled threat. *Or what?* he wanted to say. Instead, he motioned at the phone. "Someone bothering you?"

"Yes." Charles brushed him aside. "You."

Charles took the long way around to the great room and the front door, and John followed at a respectful distance, until he could sneak into the kitchen to avoid the good-byes. Lawson, hiding out in there as well, handed him a beer and they clinked bottles and stood in unison by the sink, drinking and not talking.

Perfect.

John's mind went back to a time after the kidnapping. He and Lucie working on that rundown house to turn it into a ballet studio. They'd had plenty of quiet moments together, not talking, just working. He'd shown her how to sand floors, wire new lights, and they'd painted a few walls side by side. It was easy to be with her. She didn't pry, didn't ask a million questions he couldn't answer.

She accepted him for the way he was. As least as much as

he'd told her.

Perfect.

Lucie and Zara joined them in the kitchen after seeing Charles and Olivia out. The four of them seemed to heave a collective sigh.

"Maybe you should spend the night," Lucie said to Zara. "The snow is coming fast."

Not perfect. He wanted Lucie alone.

Zara snuck a finger of frosting into her mouth. "We'll be fine. We only have to get into town where we're staying at a bed and breakfast. Tomorrow, it's Madison Avenue for shopping."

Lucie frowned. "The roads may be too snowy to get into the city."

Lawson patted Zara's stomach. "And you're supposed to be taking it easy. Doctor's orders."

"I need baby clothes! And nursery items."

There had to be sixteen boxes of exactly those things stacked in the living room from the shower.

Lawson jabbed John, obviously thinking the same thing. "Help me get that stuff out to the SUV, will you?"

John followed him and started picking up boxes. "Hey, man, if y'all want to stay here tonight, there's plenty of room."

"I know." Lawson tugged on his coat, zipped it. "Zara doesn't like it here. Bad memories or some shit. We'll be fine at the B&B. You and Lucie hang here. Have some alone time. You *are* staying, right?"

He tried not to look too eager. "Yeah. I guess so."

Lawson grinned. "Maybe you'll get snowed in."

"What if Pegasus gets called up? I'm second-in-command and you're already on vacation."

"Flynn's got it covered. CJ and the rest of the guys can handle whatever comes up."

John sighed. Flynn and CJ. A conceited spook and a crazy jarhead. Great.

"The team is covered. Relax."

He wanted to, now that he knew what was waiting for him. He wanted to give Lucie everything he could, to make her feel special for her birthday. Damn, he wished he'd known about that, so he could have bought her something.

What, he didn't know. She had everything, and from the sounds of it, was about to inherit a nice chunk of change on Monday.

Like the team they were, he and Lawson loaded the gifts, some of the leftovers, and a very pregnant Zara into Lawson's vehicle. She and Lucie hugged and promised to call each other.

And then it was just Lucie and John, watching them drive away.

FOUR

JOHN WATCHED as Lucie closed the door, set the security system, and turned to him with a nervous smile on her face. "What should we do first?"

Screw each other blind.

Whoa, boy. "Um, what do *you* want to do first?"

Her eyes widened slightly, as if she were surprised he would ask. Did she think he lacked that much control? That he would grab her and strip her naked right here in front of God and country instead of waiting for her to make the first move?

"You." She giggled.

Her assessment was spot on, then. He wasn't about to turn down that invitation.

Grabbing her, he brought her up against his body. Kissed her. Hard.

Too hard.

He didn't know what he thought she'd do. Back away? Slap him? Tell him to slow down? Beg for more? After all, she hadn't hesitated in the kitchen.

Exhaling hard, she drew back. "Give me your phone."

He scanned her face, her lips. What was she up to? "Why?"

Her answer was to crook her fingers in a *give it to me* gesture.

Whatever it took to get her naked. He fished the phone from his pocket, handed it to her.

Smiling, she walked across the floor to the fireplace and shut off the phone. Laid it on the mantel. Hers was already there. "No phones. Not this weekend."

Hardball. Now they were well and truly alone. No interruptions. No outside influences. Just her and him.

It felt weird. Being disconnected from the world and being so connected to a *person*.

Since that person was Lucie, it also felt right.

Shit. His chest tightened. For a second, he had to focus on breathing. That kind of connection was off-limits. The physical stuff? Yeah, he could handle that, welcome it with boots kicking. But that was it. He'd get her naked, get his hands and his mouth on her. Drive her wild just one more time. And then he'd stay the fuck away.

He stalked toward her. "Aren't you hot with all those clothes on?"

A repeat of the kitchen incident, she fell into his arms, going after him as fast he did her. He positioned her against the wall, hiking up the skirt of her dress with no small amount of force. He wanted her, and he was living for the here and now. Tomorrow was a long time away.

In the here and now, she wanted him, too, by the way she was kissing him back. She ripped off his shirt, for good this time, and threw it on the floor. Spread her legs and brought one of his hands down to her panties.

His fingers stroked the soft silk and she moaned, rubbing herself against him and urging his fingers on.

Happy to oblige.

He shoved the black silk down her legs until it fell on her pink shoes. A fitting contrast. Her perfect legs, his BDUs. Her manicured nails, his clean but stained ones from years in the field.

Her future as a billionaire's daughter. His past as a fucked-up redneck with no family and a chip on his shoulder.

She was going to regret this tomorrow, sure as shit. He'd rescued her from a terrorist and now she had some type of hero worship going on, but it was time to exorcise that demon once and for all. This rendezvous needed to wake her up to the reality that he didn't belong in her world, her life. He'd be nothing more than a mistake. An embarrassing mistake she'd brush under the rug at her feet when she realized he wasn't the hero she'd made him out to be.

The thought ripped at his heart. He stopped kissing her, stopped touching her. "Lucie, are you sure about this?"

Hands around his neck, she met his gaze with half-lidded, sexy eyes. He saw determination burning there.

Or was that anger flashing in those beautiful orbs? Her sigh said it was.

She was pissed? Because he'd slowed things down and took time to ask her what she wanted? He would never understand women.

Gripping his neck tighter, she drew his face to hers. "I need you, John. Now."

Okay then. Call to duty.

His fingers found the spot they sought and Lucie melted.

She said something in French he didn't understand, but didn't need to. He understood her body language, the rock of her hips, the nails digging into his skin.

A few more strokes and she whimpered. His erection jumped at the vulnerable sound. She caught his hand and moved his fingers in a quicker rhythm, her other hand cupping him through his BDUs.

Heaven.

With perfect precision and another exclamation in French, she climaxed. As she went over, arching her back, John slid a finger inside. Slick. Wet. *So perfect.*

Her body arched harder at the invasion and she clung to him, begging for more it seemed.

More it was.

Her legs sagged and he lifted her, carrying her to the immense sofa. Her shoes fell off as he walked, and he kicked off his boots as well. At the sofa, he lifted the dress over her head, fumbled with her bra as his eyes devoured her breasts. Once free, they popped into his hands and his mouth caught one, then the other, needing to taste her.

She unfastened his pants and he made quick work of losing them, letting his gaze linger on her body, naked and glowing in the light from the fire. A small, sly smile spread over her lips as he tossed off the last bits of his clothing and stood there admiring her body while his was on full display.

In a flash she moved on him, her eyes focused on his erection. Before she went down on her knees, he caught her by the wrist. "Not this time, darlin'. This time you belong to me."

Drawing him to the sofa, she lay down, spreading her legs wide. "Hard. Deep. Fast."

Orders? Was she giving *him* orders?

How about that? "Yes, ma'am. Whatever you want."

He snagged a condom from his wallet and put it on, her eyes still trained on his cock. She reached out to help roll it on, and his erection danced under her fingers. Pinning her greedy hand to her side, he climbed onto the sofa. She laughed, a light, sexy sound that filled him with a need so strong, he almost buried himself in her soft folds with one thrust. Instead, he brought the laughter to an abrupt halt by licking her breasts and then, slowly, inch by inch, pushing inside her.

She bucked, trying to make him move faster.

He stopped. She whimpered, a sound like begging, and he kissed her neck, licked it.

She moaned. More French, and he recognized a common term for please. "*S'il vous plait!*"

What he did do was sink deeper. Loving her need for him, he finally followed orders, sinking all...the...way...

Home.

Her legs went round him, clamping him tight. Her hips rose to meet his. "Oh, John."

Home. The word rattled around in his brain. He tried not to think about it. About anything but the sex.

But Lucie was so perfect beneath him, her voice so right in his ear, all he could do was think.

Lucie. Home. *My home.*

Not a place. A person.

The thought shocked him. Instinctively, he reared back. He didn't go far. Lucie's legs clamped tighter, refusing to let him go. When he looked in her eyes, the word knocked around in his brain again.

Home.

Fuck.

He didn't want a home. Didn't need one.

Didn't need anyone. Never had.

Stop thinking, he demanded of his frontal lobe. *Take no prisoners.*

He kissed her deeply, thoroughly. Began his descent again, slowing her down, forcing her to match his rhythm. Drawing himself out, he kept control of her hips, kissed her neck, tweaked a nipple.

Her eyes glazed. Was that a sheen of tears in them or was the firelight casting weird shadows?

Had he hurt her? Been too rough? Shit. "You okay?" he whispered.

"Better than okay." She confirmed it by flicking a finger over one of his nipples in return and trailing kisses down his neck. "But I need more."

Ordering him around again. He was starting to like it. He released her wrist, reached between them, and touched her. Right. *There.*

Bingo. She whimpered and the sexy sound made him realize he was close. Too close. But she was, too. Maybe it was time to give the lady what she wanted.

He drove himself in, ramping up his touch at the same time. She moved in perfect sync with him, eyes still open and watching. "Harder."

Out. In. Lucie's sweet heat taking him fully. Releasing and begging for more.

Another retreat. Another advance.

"John—"

Bam, she exploded. Gritting his teeth to hold back his own release, he rode the orgasm with her, milking it. After a few seconds, she looked at him, spread her legs wider, and breathed softly. "Come for me."

Another order. One he couldn't help but follow. Finally letting go of his control, he came in a rush, blinding and perfect in its pleasure.

Lust and another feeling, warm and inviting, crashed together, taking the edge off the anger always riding him. Freeing him from the past. Planting a seed of hope for the future.

Home.

Slowing his breathing, he blocked the thought, closed his

eyes and drifted, buoyed on the sound of Lucie's breath, the feel of her under him.

Wrapping her in his arms, he shifted their bodies to take his weight off her.

She snuggled into his chest. "*Le petit mort*," she murmured with a sigh. "So good."

He might have been from Texas, but he knew what that particular French idiom meant. *The little death*. The moment of release.

With a shock, He realized he'd just released more than months of sexual frustration over her. More than anger over, well, everything else in his life stemming from his past. More, in fact, than he could identify.

His heart felt lighter. His brain, calmer.

Rubbing her back, he smiled into the shadows that had fallen during their lovemaking, the coming hours stretching out in front of him like a shiny, new coin dying to be spent. As the fire burned, the sound of the crackling wood cocooning them, he let his body totally relax. Just for this moment, this weekend, he was happy.

And he liked it.

When she moved against him a few minutes later, he kissed her, caressed her breasts, and nuzzled her neck.

He was ready for his next set of orders.

FIVE

John stood at the master suite window early the next morning looking down on his truck. The familiar itch burning under his skin told him it was time to leave. The pain knotting itself like a rope in his chest when he considered it said different. *No way, don't be a royal dick, you loser.*

He'd gone out to the truck to retrieve his overnight bag and found himself hesitating at the door. So easy to jump in and drive away. Definite dick move, but old habits died damned hard.

But he didn't want to. Now he stared at the footprints in the snow leading back and forth and thought about Lucie. Every time he walked away from her, he ended up coming back.

Maybe for a good reason.

In the adjacent bathroom, the shower came on. Her voice called to him over the noise, "What do you want for breakfast?"

The image of Lucie, warm and wet under the hot water, made his body harden. "You," he answered.

She laughed. "You like eggs, yes? I brought bacon, too."

Who would've thought he'd still be here, talking about something as ordinary as what to have for breakfast? All night they'd talked and laughed and fucked, that same easiness between them that John had never felt with another woman.

An easiness that scared him.

Yet, here he was, discussing breakfast options. Outside, his lonely truck sat in a bed of dazzling snow. It would take an hour to unbury it, clear off the drive. Meanwhile, the nasty blizzard raged, daring him to try.

But it was nothing compared to the storm inside his heart.

A smart man would hightail it to the shower, grab the soap, and wash her back and all those other body parts he loved so much. A smart man would go cook the eggs and bacon and work hard to make her laugh again.

But then, a smart man would enjoy the way she looked at him all the time with her heart in her eyes. Those beautiful, emotion-filled eyes. She was hungry for love, not just sex, and while he'd pretended it didn't matter, it did.

Shit. Why was he still here?

Because once I had her in front of me again, once I tasted her lips and heard those words—John, I need *you—I couldn't let her go. I couldn't leave.*

Not this time.

Running away was for pussies. In the line of duty, he'd never run from anything. In his private life, it was just the opposite. He was tired of running from people, from his own fucking emotions. Maybe with Lucie he didn't have to.

Home.

He glanced at his buried ride again. The freedom it offered suddenly didn't appeal.

Wandering over to the open bathroom door, he took a deep breath. Leaned on the jamb. He didn't have to leave. He could stay, explore this thing with Lucie —whatever it was—and not panic.

"Eggs and bacon would be perfect," he said, watching her through the frosted glass. Simple, ordinary conversation the morning after. A first for him.

He liked it.

"I'll make some scones, too," she said, washing her hair. She leaned back into the water stream, her breasts on glorious display behind the glass.

John's cock twitched, but he stayed rooted where he was, forcing himself to soak in this seemingly mundane moment of "normal." The type of normal he'd never had.

Was this what Lawson had with Zara?

John's chest still felt tight, and the itch to leave lingered under his skin, but normal wasn't as bad as he'd expected. In fact, he felt...content.

Another first.

Lost in his thoughts, he was surprised when the shower shut off. Lucie opened the door, grabbed a towel, and stepped out. When she saw his face, her brows knit into a frown. "If you don't like scones, I'll make toast."

"Um...sure." He tried to concentrate on the breakfast selection, but all he could think about was how much he wanted to freeze this moment. "Lucie?"

She toweled her wet hair, the frown dissipating. "Yes?"

Standing still, he just stared at her, trying to work out what he'd been thinking. Wanting to tell her that he was staying, that he hoped to stay longer than breakfast. Longer, maybe, than the weekend.

He started to speak, stopped. *Tell her.*

Wrapping the towel around her body, she noticed his struggle and her eyes grew wary. "What is it?"

His jaw clamped tight as a vise, refusing to let the words out.

She stepped toward him. "*Ça va?* Are you okay?"

Backing up, he shook his head. No, he wasn't fucking okay. The ragged knot was back in his chest, tight as a bitch. He was stupid, foolish.

Scared.

Don't be a pussy.

"I'm... I want to..." Jesus. What was wrong with him?

Her face fell, the light in her eyes dimming. "You're leaving then? Before breakfast?"

The hurt in her voice was too much. Way too much. They'd been here before—him bailing—so what else did she expect? He turned, faced the wall, wanting to put his fist in it.

This was why he couldn't do relationships. Not all the other bullshit he told himself. It wasn't his job or the fact he could be killed on any of his missions and leave behind a family. He was broken inside. Something wasn't right. Other people knew how to handle emotions, knew how to tell another person they loved and cared about them. He didn't.

Lucie came up behind him, touched him lightly on the arm. "It's okay. I understand."

"Just..." Shit, she thought he was leaving again. He had to find the words. Whatever it took. "Give me a second, Luce. I'm okay. I just need a fucking second."

She had to be so confused, God knew he was, but she simply wrapped her arms around him and laid her head on his bare shoulder. "You can have all the time you need. I'm not going anywhere."

Not going anywhere. *No more running.*

Turning in her arms, John grabbed her face and covered her mouth with his. Once more, he felt her acceptance, her understanding. He needed to convey what he felt, not with words, but with actions.

Her mouth was warm and soft, letting him take control. His hands went to the edge of the towel, and as his lips worked her mouth, his fingers slipped the towel free, sending it to the floor.

Breaking the kiss, he spoke against her lips. "I need you, Lucie."

A heartbeat of silence. "You're *not* leaving?"

Taking her face in his hands again, he simply shook his head. Then he went back to kissing her, devouring her, teasing his way into her mouth.

Her hands skimmed his chest, one dropping down to tickle the waistband of his sweatpants and delving inside. It fisted around his hard cock and he moaned, kissing her deeper and nearly laughing with relief as the crazy lust flared between them like always.

He *would* talk to her. After breakfast. He'd tell her he wanted to try and make something out of this. Something more than sex and a weekend fling. He would...just not right now.

Right now, there was a blizzard going on, he had a woman to please, and hours and hours of uninterrupted time in which to do it.

SIX

LUCIE WOKE in John's arms and reveled in the feel of him. In the smell of him. For the first time in weeks—maybe months— she relaxed.

They'd made love so many times, she'd lost count. Brought many of her fantasies to life. Ate cold leftovers, played naked pool, and took a swim. Both exhausted after all the fun and games, they'd gone to bed late yesterday afternoon and stayed there.

She grinned at the memory. Cuddling deeper into the lush blankets, warm with John's natural heat, she was bone tired from all the physical activity, but her heart was full. His nearness, the feel of his arms around her, filled her with an even deeper level of contentment.

She'd been so convinced he would leave after the first night. Surprisingly, he'd stayed. Was it her directness? The support she'd offered? Or just the sex?

Dismissing that thought, reassurance came when she remembered John saying how much this meant to him—the way she'd set up this weekend retreat. He appreciated her. The sex was amazing, but there was something deeper going on here, and they both knew it.

Midnight was half an hour away. She'd dreamed about her birthday and all the things on her bucket list the trust fund could help her mark off. That list and the money could do a lot of good in the world.

But the millions going into her bank account in a few minutes couldn't compete with the way John made her feel. She prayed they'd have more than this weekend to relive in the coming weeks and months. Out of the blue, he'd tossed out an idea that maybe they could head south for a few days together. Spend the rest of his leave where it was warm and sunny.

Her heart had jumped at the suggestion...not because she hated winter, but because he was making plans with her. *Real* plans. Commitment. He was no longer trying to get away, or refusing to talk about his feelings. Not that he was an open book yet, she wasn't sure he ever would be. It wasn't his style. Yet, they'd definitely made progress.

He moved against her, tucking her in closer. "You awake?"

"*Oui.*" No need to ask the same of him. His erection pressed against her bottom. "I love waking in your arms."

He nuzzled her neck and she shivered. "Glad I stayed. Wasn't sure your dad was going to let me."

Outside the windows, the moon reflected off the snow-covered ground. Two long stripes of blue light fell across the king-size bed. Lucie turned in his arms to face him, loving the way the diffused light accentuated his strong jaw and muscled shoulder. "I wasn't sure he would let either of us. Zara insisted and he gave in. Like he always does with her."

"From what I've seen, she gets her way with everyone." They both smiled at that. "It's good you and Z are tight."

Zara felt like the only real family she had here. "The truth about Charles being my father didn't come out until we were nearly teens. No one believed it except Zara. The DNA test proved the truth, but did nothing to endear me to them. I gave up the idea of becoming a Morgan for a long time. Zara and I remained close, though. Each of us longed for a sister growing up, so the day we found out about each other, it was...*du bon et du mauvais*. Good and bad. How do you say it? A mixed blessing?"

"Had plenty of those in my life."

A wonderful memory came back to her. The first time Zara had phoned her. Lucie had been in Paris; Zara lived in New York with Charles and Olivia. "From the moment we met, I wanted to be just like her. She was going to be a great ballerina, like her mother, and I was jealous. My mother worked in a factory sewing clothes."

"You weren't rich?"

"Far from it!"

John snorted. "Grass is always greener, right?"

Lucie's heart warmed at being able to finally talk to him about her sister. In their brief times together, John had steered away from discussions about family. "A few years later, Zara was injured. At the same time I was offered a modeling contract. Our situations reversed. We grew even closer. I hated it that she had to give up ballet."

"But she was happy for you, I bet."

"Very much so. Of course, she's an overachiever. Had to show me up by becoming a spy."

They both chuckled. "Do you miss modeling?"

Different responses tumbled through her head. "Some days, yes. Most, no. The experience was amazing on many levels. Something lots of girls dream of, you know? For me, I enjoyed traveling and seeing so many places. Meeting many people. Seeing myself all made up. Walking runways...it's quite a life. I missed my mother though. Still do."

He scratched at the stubble on his chin. "Do you plan to visit her anytime soon?"

"I can't wait for her to see the studio! She's coming here in February. We see each other as often as possible, text constantly, and FaceTime every week. She's always been my rock. Once my trust fund is available, I'll pay off her debts and she can quit work if she wants to. She's quite a cook, and to be honest, I'd love to help her buy a place to have her own café."

"Sounds cool. How is the ballet studio?"

After Dmitri, Zara had conned Charles into giving her money to open a dance studio for underprivileged kids. Lucie became her partner, running the place while Zara was out of town on her secret missions. Lucie had discovered she liked being in charge of something. Plus, she loved kids. The only down side was it reminded her every day of her ticking clock. Would she ever be a mother?

In the early days, the kids had taken Lucie's mind off her own problems and given her perspective. They still did, and it was welcome. "We have so many applications! I plan to hire two extra instructors next week and set up additional after-school classes by April. This summer, I'm adding drama classes, music lessons, and modeling training. I have a lot of connections from my modeling days, and my trust fund money is going to help more kids. Most of them are awful at ballet, but a few have potential to go into other types of entertainment."

He smiled. Brushed a strand of hair from her face. "Most women about to inherit that kind of dough would be thinking about jewelry, shoes, and weekend getaways to St. Tropez."

"I have been to St. Tropez on a shoot. Beautiful, but I've always wanted to visit Disneyland. Have you ever been?"

John's face contorted and he barked a laugh. "Never, but I hear it's nice. Maybe that's where we'll go while I'm on vacation."

"I would like that. Besides, I don't wear much jewelry and I have plenty of shoes. Some of the kids we help have nothing."

"You know..." He hesitated as if struggling with himself. His fingers lingered on her neck. "You're too good for this family."

Shocked, she drew back. "Not true, John. Charles is a philanthropist, donating thousands of dollars every year to worthy causes, and Zara—"

"Z's a lot like you. She cares about other people. Your ol' man? Sorry, darlin', but the only reason he gives away money is so he can write it off and look good doing it."

"Write it off?"

"His taxes. And he's in the tax bracket that pays a lot less than the working man."

Lucie shook her head. "You don't know him."

"I know men *like* him." He raked a hand over his face. "You don't need his approval, Luce."

She chewed her bottom lip. On some level, she was still the little girl without a father in her life. "I just want to have a family. A *real* family."

"Why?"

Was he really asking her that? "Everyone wants to be loved, to be part of a family. Don't you?"

John rolled onto his back, stared up at the ceiling. Didn't answer.

There it was again. She'd said something wrong. "Lawson told me you don't have any family."

"Lawson should keep his trap shut." He heaved a sigh. "Pegasus is my family. Before that, it was my Delta Force brothers."

"What about blood relations?"

"Don't know who my father was, and my mother was a junkie who gave me up at birth. I bounced around in foster homes until I ended up in front of a judge at seventeen. He offered me a choice: the army or jail. Best father figure I ever had."

Sadness tugged at her heart. She wanted to tell him she was sorry, but from dealing with the kids like him at the studio, she knew he'd see it as pity. There was no room in John for that. He'd hate it. "A mixed blessing then, yes? If you hadn't chosen the army, we never would have met. You served your country, and saved dozens of people during your time with Team Pegasus. People like me."

He put an arm behind his head. "Some days that's enough. Some days..."

He trailed off and Lucie frowned. "What do you mean?"

"Nothing."

Nothing translated to the failures of his latest missions, she would bet. That she understood. She also understood he wasn't ready to talk about them.

Laying her hand on his chest, she traced the outline of his tattoo. "What does it mean?"

He glanced down, followed her finger with his eyes. "Some kind of endless knot or luck symbol. It's Buddhist, I think."

"You don't know the meaning of your tattoo?"

"Not really." A grin tugged at the corner of his mouth. "Got it a long time ago when I was still a Beret undercover in Indonesia. We were looking for a gang leader, so I went drinking with some of his boys. Befriended them, you know, and ended up with this tattoo and a hell of a hangover."

What a life he'd led. "I'd like to hear more of your stories."

He glanced at her, looked away.

"If they are not..." What had he called it? Zara worked these types of missions. There was secret, top secret and... "Classified."

He came up on his elbow, stroked her arm. "You're amazing, Lucie. I want you to know that I, uh, I..."

Overhead, a *thud* sounded. Then another.

Lucie glanced up. "What was that?"

John looked at the ceiling as if he had x-ray vision. "Tree branch, probably. Everything's covered with the heavy snowfall."

They fell silent, listening. The wind blew and the house grew quiet. John kissed her and she kissed him back, wondering what it was he wanted her to know.

They were getting hot and heavy when a faint *squeak, squeak, squeak* came from downstairs.

John tensed in mid-kiss. He raised his head.

Squeak, squeak, squeak.

Lucie strained her ears. "Is that the refrigerator?"

His focus went to the bedroom door. "You set the security system, right?"

Had she? So much had happened since the party, her memory was a blur. "I believe so."

A nerve jumped in John's jaw.

"You think someone's trying to break in?"

"After this storm? Nah." He flipped back the sheets, pulled on a pair of sweatpants. Rummaged in his overnight bag and stuck something black in his pocket. "Probably the fridge like you said. I'll go check."

She could read him too well. He didn't believe it was the refrigerator.

Rising hastily, she grabbed one of his shirts from the floor. "I'll come with you."

"No." His ear was against the bedroom door and he looked over his shoulder. "You stay here. It's probably nothing. I'll be back in a minute."

No way. She was going with him. But a drop of fear entered her bloodstream. Fear—the emotion she hated most.

John slipped out the door. "Lock this behind me."

Lock it? The fear spread. "John—"

"It's okay." He smiled, but his body language said it was *not* okay. "I'm just being paranoid."

Paranoia. Her constant unwanted companion for months after leaving Paris. "Better safe than sorry, yes?"

With a nod, he shut the door. Lucie crossed the room and laid a hand on the lock. This was ridiculous. Houses always made weird noises at night. The blizzard might be over but the wind was still blowing hard. That could be the cause.

She locked the door anyway. Refusing to give in to senseless fear, she backed away and sat on the bed. Then she flipped on the bedside lamp.

Nothing happened.

The power was out. Luckily, the house had a backup generator. It would kick on momentarily.

A minute passed. Deep in the bowels of the house, she heard a motor start. The light came on and Lucie breathed a sigh of relief.

Another minute and she heard nothing downstairs.

No John.

Waiting sucked. Especially when adrenaline whooshed through her veins, demanding she do *some*thing. Anything. The bad memories from her abduction and torture at Dmitri's hands crawled like scorpions through her brain. Her limbs trembled.

The bedroom had a fireplace. Although it was gas, it looked like a traditional log-burning unit like the one downstairs. It even had a set of iron accessories. Bolting for them, she grabbed the poker, tapped the solid iron against her palm.

Better safe than sorry. That was an American idiom she fully understood.

Returning to the bed, she plunked down with her weapon. Endless hours of therapy had helped her control her fear of being a victim, but when confronted with the real possibility once more, the therapy, she discovered, was flat-out worthless.

John's here. Nothing bad would happen when he was around.

She kept a tight hold on the iron poker and watched the door.

SEVEN

THE SQUEAK of wet shoes on the marble floor gave away the intruder's presence.

John pressed his back against the living room wall next to a portrait of Charles and Olivia and froze. That's what he'd heard upstairs: the unmistakable sound of wet boot treads on a dry surface.

Easing forward on bare feet, he brought the massive front door into view. There were no lights on downstairs. None except for a light on the security panel that told him the system was activated. How had the intruder gotten in?

For a second, John hoped it was Lawson who'd come back because Zara had forgotten something. *Lawson would've announced himself. Lawson would've waited until daylight.*

A dark shadow outside the expanse of front windows caught his eye. Clouds had moved across the moon again, but snow lit the landscape, turning the dark lake a bluish white.

Except where the tracks of a vehicle had disturbed the snow.

Who the fuck would be out in this storm?

John recognized the tracks—a four-wheeler. One that had pulled something behind it. A cart? A wagon?

The footsteps in the kitchen fell quiet, but the distinct presence of another human radiated in the stillness. Was the intruder a survivalist nut who'd gotten lost in the storm and sought shelter?

John glanced at the security light. A stranded person would have knocked and rang the doorbell. If they'd broken in, the security system would have gone off.

Which led him back to the idea the person had a key, knew the security system code.

One of the Morgan family? He couldn't see them traveling in anything but their fancy cars, and definitely not in this kind of weather.

He edged toward the fireplace. The fire was long out, the embers cold. His cell phone and Lucie's lay on the mantel. He snatched up both, turning his on, and pocketing hers.

He kept his phone on silent all the time, a habit born of being in compromising situations in the field. The bars showed no service. Not surprising in this area under the current weather conditions.

He touched an icon on the screen that appeared like a normal app and his phone transformed into the Agency-enhanced computer it was. The extra juice stored inside the phone amped its ability to find a cell tower. After typing in his password, he went through a series of screens and found a list of available Wi- Fi connections in service that could link him to a specific satellite. Once it connected, he sent a message to Lawson: *Trouble brewing. May need backup.*

What kind of trouble was the question. Boot treads. A four-wheeler. A quiet intruder who had bypassed a high-end security alarm to do a B&E during a blizzard.

Only a few types of people could or would pull that off. And they weren't your garden-variety survivalists.

Military. Special ops. Assassins.

None of which made him happy, but...

A military or spec ops soldier would never give himself away by the sound of his boots. An assassin smart enough to bypass a security system? *Puh-lease.*

John had to operate under that assumption anyway. Whoever the mystery visitor was, he was good. Just not as good as John.

Need to get eyes on him.

Passing the fireplace, he took slow, measured steps. In his line of work, he'd pissed off a lot of people. Most never knew his real name, who he worked for, or where he lived. Half of them never saw him; Pegasus typically got in and out without raising an eyebrow. Missions were classified, all labeled secret or top secret. Details limited to a handful of people directly involved with the logistics or the outcome. The CIA, FBI, DoD—they had knowledge of the jobs, but only the person giving the orders knew the names of the operatives with boots on the ground.

Despite that, there were always leaks, and people like Lucie who knew the truth.

Now her family knew, too. There'd been no away around that when she and Zara had been kidnapped by Dmitri.

The Russians, the Mexicans, the Afghans, hell, a common criminal...didn't matter who was in the house. John had a job to do.

Protect Lucie. Neutralize the enemy.

John palmed his gun. Thanks to his and Lucie's escapades during the weekend, he knew the layout of the house like the back of his hand. Did the intruder? If the man knew the code for the huge cabin, he knew the layout.

What had he carried in the cart? Was the intruder a highly-skilled burglar who planned to abscond with some of the Morgan family's expensive collections?

Was there more than one person? Did they know the house was occupied?

Were they armed?

Questions continued to bombard him as he scooted to the corner, took a steadying breath with both hands on the gun, his finger on the trigger. Raising the weapon, he peeked around the corner into the kitchen.

The table was empty except for a scattering of cake and icing. They hadn't cleaned anything up from the party, the chairs pushed out of the way and the island sporting a jumble of trays and plates. A few decorations Lucie had torn down were piled in one corner.

No one in sight.

John's gaze bounced over the outline of dirty champagne glasses by the sink, passed over the various appliances... came back to the island.

A silhouette caught his attention. Darker than the rest, it was a black square amidst the clutter. A tiny light on the side pulsed on and off.

A laptop.

Not his. Not Lucie's.

Their guest had set it up and left it here. John held his breath and listened. Where had the intruder gone? He looked up, wishing he could see the second floor and assure himself Lucie was safe.

As if in response, a shot rang out.

Lucie screamed.

EIGHT

THE NIGHTMARE WAS HAPPENING ALL OVER AGAIN. The bad nightmare. The *really* bad one.

Locked doors had never kept the nightmare away before, and they didn't this time either.

The door, lock blown to bits by a bullet, swung open. A man in a black ski mask pointed a gun at her head. Screaming, she jumped up, adrenaline pumping through her veins like wild fire, and took a good, hard swing at him.

But his friend, another goon in a gray ski mask, jumped forward and blocked her arm. He ripped the poker out of her hand and sent her sprawling to the floor.

"John!"

The man in black stepped forward and she could just make out the smile on his lips under the mask. "You're even prettier than I thought. Get up."

Keeping her focus on the gun, Lucie rose as instructed. Black Mask moved behind her, motioned at the second man to toss him the poker.

Before she could fight back, he wrapped an arm around her

neck and jerked her back against his chest. Jamming the long, cold poker iron across her throat, he gave a tug. The hard iron bit into her skin, cutting off oxygen. The pain was terrifying, an odd pressure that told her the tiniest slip and her windpipe could be crushed.

The pressure on her windpipe intensified. Tiny black dots danced at the edges of her vision. The second man looked over his shoulder and slipped into the shadows behind the open door.

John appeared a second later, his attention landing on her, as he calmly walked into view. His eyes were flat and hard, but all she felt was relief. *John will stop this.*

Glancing at the masked assailant holding her, he raised his hands in surrender.

No, no, no. Lucie tried to say his name, but what came out was an odd sound and fresh pain burst in her throat. What was he doing?

He stepped into the room and the goon holding her forced her back a step. John stopped.

His voice was low and composed—as if this kind of thing happened every day. "Yo, man. Whoever you are, you want me, not her, so don't hurt her, okay? Release her and we'll talk."

Black Mask chuckled in her ear. It sounded weird, mechanized almost. "Wrong. Your girlfriend is way more valuable than you."

Lucie tried to catch John's eyes. He was totally focused on the man. She darted a glance to the other guy behind the door and frantically pointed in that direction, trying to warn John he was there.

Black Mask yanked on her, taking another step back. More pain exploded along her windpipe, and her feet got tangled. Roughly, he righted her and smacked her bare leg with the unforgiving poker. He shoved her toward the bed, and at the same time, the second man emerged from behind the door and pointed a gun at John's head.

"John!" she screamed.

He ducked and pivoted, grabbing Gray Mask in a bear hug and jamming him against the wall. That man's gun went off and plaster rained from the ceiling.

Fresh pain bloomed in her back where her captor whipped her with the hard metal. She dropped to the floor on hands and knees, the bed blocking her view of John and his fight. Desperate, she attempted to climb over it. Black Mask grabbed her by the hair and yanked her off, her knees hitting hard on the floor.

Anger and fear made her lash out once more, attacking the man. He seemed somewhat surprised at her viciousness and lost his balance slightly. When he swung the poker this time, she grabbed it, a sharp sting bursting to life in her palm.

As John knocked the gun out of his assailant's hand, Lucie stomped on Black Mask's foot. His gun made another appearance, the cold, hard end of the pistol suddenly lodging under her left ear.

She froze.

"Enough!" he yelled, his voice still sounding unnatural. It reminded her of a television documentary she'd seen with Zara where the person interviewed had their voice changed to remain anonymous. "Or I shoot the girl."

John stopped dead. Seeing the gun, he released the other man. Slowly, he raised his hands and faced Black Mask. "Relax. Whatever it is you want, we'll work it out."

Where was John's gun? She was sure that's what he'd put in his pocket earlier, but she hadn't seen it during the fight.

The man in the gray mask slumped to the floor, coughing and gagging. Lucie could relate. Her windpipe burned and her voice had sounded ragged when she'd yelled John's name.

Thank God he was calm. She was shaking like the wind-blown leaves outside the windows. Black Mask had said he wanted her. Was he one of Dmitri's men come to the States to kill her out of spite?

John made a *lower the gun* motion with his hand. "Take the weapon away from her head. You don't want to hurt her."

"Shut up." Black Mask put an arm around her shoulders, pushed the end of the gun into her skull. There was no European accent leaking through the mechanized sound, now that she was attuned to it. He wasn't one of Dmitri's, but maybe someone they'd hired? "Lucie and I have business to discuss."

The second man rose on hands and knees, coughing. John ignored him. "What kind of business?"

Lucie wanted to know, too, but a part of her didn't care. The nightmare was back. She'd fought it, but it hadn't worked. All she cared about was getting out of this alive. Getting *John* out of this alive.

John had given her a hostage negotiating lesson when she'd asked how Pegasus had rescued her and Zara. She still remembered what he'd said: *Find out what they want. Find a way to give it to them. Get something in return.*

Lucie tried to stop shaking and sound like she knew what she was doing. "What is it you want with me?"

"Cuff him," Black Mask said to his partner. "Relieve him of his weapon and put him in the wine cellar."

That wasn't the answer she was looking for.

The accomplice staggered to his feet, recovered his gun and pointed it at John. His voice was hollow-sounding and scratchy. "How about I kill him? He's nothing to us."

Oh, God, no. "What do you *want*?" Lucie demanded again, panic hitting her low in her stomach. "You said this was about me, so leave him out of it."

Black Mask rubbed the side of her face with his, the knit

mask rough against her skin. "All in due time. Fifteen minutes, to be exact."

John let the second man pull his hands behind his back and restrain them with a couple of plastic straps. Lucie knew those straps. Dmitri's men had used the same kind on her when they'd drugged her and tied her to a bed.

Fifteen minutes. Lucie glanced at the blue numbers of the bedside clock. A bitter tension slid down her spine. "My trust fund? You want my money?"

The second man snickered as he patted John down and took the weapon he found hidden in John's sweatpants. He tossed it on the bed. "Your girlfriend catches on fast."

Black Mask gave Lucie's hair a tug, tipping her head back and revealing her neck. "Your father owes me a debt." He ran the tip of the gun over her vulnerable skin. "And I'm here to collect."

"Her father will pay a ransom," John reasoned. "I can call him for you."

"Always the hero, aren't you, Quick?"

He knew who John was? Icy blackness threatened to take Lucie under.

Black Mask released her hair, but kept her snug against him, the gun jammed once more under her ear. "There won't be any ransom. I know how that works out for the kidnapper. Seen it up close and personal. Usually I don't have to get my hands dirty, but a simple hack job to relieve Charles Morgan of his money would be too...anticlimactic. No, this job requires me and Lucie to enjoy each other while we screw over her father."

"I don't know what you're talking about," Lucie ground out. She kept her eyes pinned on John. Her stomach threatened to revolt, black dots swimming around the edges of her vision. "But whatever my father's done to offend you, I'm sorry."

Black Mask laughed like it was all a big joke. "Offend me?"

The laugher died away. He gave her a jerk, put his lips to her ear. "He fucking killed my mother. An eye for an eye, I say. Nothing means more to him than his money. And his daughters."

The man was insane. Just like Dmitri.

Lucie held John's gaze. *Find a way to give them what they want. Get something in return.* It took all of her resolve not to let the darkness win its creeping advance on her. The muscles in her body frozen with fear. "Take my trust fund. Take it all. When the money hits my account, I'll have it wired to whatever offshore account you want...if, and *only* if, you release John."

He paused, shook his head as if she were an errant school-child, the scratchy mask tickling her cheek. "Negotiating?" He tapped the gun against her temple. "Neither you nor Quick are in a position to negotiate with me, now are you, Ms. Morgan?"

Her teeth threatened to chatter. She clenched her jaw.

John, still appearing calm, tried to reason with him. "Kill Lucie and you won't get your money."

"Oh, I'll get it. But this way, I get to have a little fun, too." He motioned to his partner. "Get him out of here and bring me my laptop."

Gray Mask led John out of the bedroom.

Lucie's hope of saving him and surviving this went with them.

NINE

JOHN WENT QUIETLY, letting the guy push and prod him down the stairs as he walked too slowly for the guy's liking. With his hands secured behind his back, keeping his balance wasn't easy, so he bounced off the railing a few times, lost his footing and sat down on a step. Anything to stall while he figured out how he knew the leader of this little escapade.

Not military or special ops, although the guy had military-like training.

Definitely not an assassin, although he had the moves and the lingo of a kidnapper.

The way he'd wielded the poker in his right hand and the gun in his left took skill.

He knew my name.

FBI? CIA? Pegasus technically worked for JSOC and ran foreign missions for the CIA because of their training and qualifications. Because of that, John knew spooks inside and out, but this guy...

I know how that works out for the kidnapper. Seen it up close and personal.

Experienced with kidnappers. FBI?

The leader's partner—the one kicking and shoving John down the steps—was the muscle of the operation. Nothing military about him, but he'd probably had police or security guard training.

A Bureau agent kidnapping someone? Hell of a deal. The perfect deal, in fact. Guy would know exactly how to avoid getting caught and he'd most likely already gained access to everything about John and Lucie, right down to the cabin's security code.

The idea made John's blood run hot.

Criminals existed in all branches of the government; the FBI wasn't immune. John Connelly had been convicted of racketeering and obstruction of justice. Robert Hanssen had sold U.S. secrets to the Russians and Soviets for twenty- two years. There were a handful of other Bureau employees who'd been convicted over the years.

FBI guy had mentioned hacking and a laptop. The laptop had to be the one John had seen on the kitchen island.

Muscle walked him through the living room and into the kitchen, gun pointed at John's back. As they passed the island, John pretended to trip, knocking his elbow into the laptop. It skidded to the side, taking out a few plates and crashing to the marble floor.

The captor flipped on the overhead lights. "Asshole." He picked up the laptop and moved to John's side, swinging the butt of the gun at John's head. John ducked, kicked out with his right foot, and nailed the guy in the shin.

Muscle swung again, losing his balance but managing to make contact with John's temple.

Stung like a bitch. John leveraged his weight, falling into the guy and knocking him off balance. The laptop smacked into the counter, and using the momentum of his body, John rotated and landed a kick to the guy's wrist.

The gun flew sideways, bouncing off a cabinet and skittering across the floor.

A voice from the second floor interrupted the fight. "What the hell's going on down there, Mattock?"

Mattock shot John a rage-filled look as he set the laptop on the table. If the leader was calling Mattock by name in front of them, it meant John and Lucie were not walking out of the cabin alive. "Nothing, boss," the guy called back. "Everything's under control."

"Hurry up with the laptop."

"Yes, sir."

They waited for the footsteps to retreat overhead before they both went for the gun at the same time, John diving and twisting his body to block him as Mattock also dove forward, hand outstretched. John head-butted him and got kneed in the balls for his trouble.

Mattock rolled, cursing and holding his head. Going fetal, John used his body to conceal the gun, which had slid under a chair.

John caught his breath and angled a foot beneath the chair. He kicked the gun hard and sent it under the long wooden table and into the kitchen's far corner. As he rolled over to come up on his knees, a sharp object sliced into his left side.

Red-hot pain tore through skin and muscle, the blade driving deep into his back and leaving him gasping for breath. He nearly belly-flopped from the searing torment.

"How'd'ya like that, asshole?"

Shit. What had Mattock stuck him with? A K-bar? Steak knife? God, that much pain could *not* come from a wimpy ol' steak knife...

Warm blood trickled down John's back, ran into his waist-band. Fucker was going to pay for that.

If John could stand up, which at the moment was proving difficult. The aftermath of the one-two to his groin and kidney made his stomach flip upside down.

He stood up anyway, faced the bastard.

The cake server was in the man's hand.

Aw, fuck. Icing clung to the silver. Blood dripped from the serrated edge. The man was breathing hard and had a welt on his forehead.

John thought he might pass out. But not before he got in one more assault. "Give up yet, pussy?"

The term threw Mattock off for a split second, and that's all John needed. Lowering his head, he gut-rammed him, a bull in full charge, slamming the enemy into the cabinet.

Mattock didn't drop the cake server, but his spine slammed the countertop hard enough to illicit a heavy grunt. By the time he recovered and lashed out with the cake server again, John had already dropped, locked his legs around the man's ankles and yanked.

Mattock's knees gave out, feet lurching up in the air. On his way down, he tried to twist away and head-smacked the corner of the countertop.

A sickening thud echoed in the kitchen and Mattock's head snapped back. Slowly, his limp body slid down and toppled over, unconscious. *Ting!* The cake server hit the floor.

Mr. FBI upstairs had to have heard the commotion. Moving as fast as his injuries allowed, John shimmied across the floor and maneuvered the handle of the kitchen implement-turned weapon between his palms. With small, quick flicks back and forth, he sawed through part of the flexicuffs binding his wrists. If his arms had been bound in front, he could have broken the cuffs with extreme pressure. He'd done it before. Behind his back, though? He couldn't overpower them unless they were already compromised.

Compromised plastic coming up. The tension eased as the server worked. A sharp tug of his wrists and he was free.

Mattock had no pulse. Fucker was dead.

Good.

The leader of the two-man crew yelled from the second floor again. Staggering to his feet, John ran his fingers around the wound in his lower back and ignored the too-loud pounding of his pulse in his ears. His hand came away covered in blood. As he retrieved the phones from the drawer he'd hidden them in before running upstairs, the edges of his vision swam.

He had to get to Lucie, but he'd be worthless if he passed out first.

Passing out seemed likely. Shock from the loss of blood was creeping in fast. Cool skin, back pain, flank pain, extreme tenderness over his kidney.

In the field, John had treated a lot of abdominal and back injuries. Fucking Mattock might have nicked his kidney. Hard to do, but serious shit if John didn't stop the bleeding.

He hauled out his phone, hit a button that would send an SOS to Langley. Doubtful Del Hoffman was around this time of night, but the SOS would get answered by someone. Pegasus would kick into action.

Vision swimming, he snatched up a cotton dishtowel monogramed with a fancy M and pressed the embroidered letter to his bleeding wound. His assailant had a nice, wide, black belt around his pants that would work for the tourniquet. John stumbled over to where the guy lay, sank to his knees, and went to work removing the belt, as he heard the leader of the two-man crew yell from upstairs.

Hurry. He nearly keeled over from the pain and lightheadedness. The memory of Lucie with a gun to her head revived him.

He glanced at the kitchen doorway. Listened for footsteps. Where was Mr. FBI? Why hadn't he come down to check on his buddy and find out what all the noise was?

John's brain felt like it was filled with cotton candy. The only answer it supplied made him want to throw up.

The guy hadn't come down to find out what was going on because the bastard was too busy torturing Lucie.

TEN

"Mattock!" Black Mask stood in the upstairs hallway yelling for his partner.

Lucie, located in front of him, stared down the long, curving stairs to the first floor. She swallowed hard.

John's okay. He *had* to be okay.

A frigid deadness had crept into her heart when she'd seen John led away, hands cuffed behind his back. If anything happened to him...

She'd heard the noises downstairs as the man behind her had been taunting her. Saw how he'd gotten nervous, even as he'd plucked at her clothes, explained in great detail how he was going to torture her.

Her own nerves were strung tight. "Your partner's dead," she blurted. She could hope, right? "You will be soon as well."

He shoved her, sending her sprawling down several steps. "Shut up, bitch."

Gaining her balance, she continued the rest of the way down with slow steps, thinking of ways to get that gun away from him. Her hands were free. She could run. Or attack him. Or...

Or what, Lucie?

The living room was dark except for a slice of light coming from the kitchen. In the back of her mind, her worst fear had been that she'd be in this exact situation. That she'd be the victim again.

Now her worst fear was seeing John hurt. Or dead.

As they rounded the corner to the kitchen, Lucie's heart stopped.

The place was a wreck and there was blood everywhere. Too much blood. "John?"

He was slumped in the corner of the kitchen behind the long table. The table where they'd made love. The table where a laptop sat.

Heedless of Black Mask's gun, she ran to John, falling on her knees. His eyes were closed, his waist encircled with a belt. Bright red blood covered his entire side. "*Mon Dieu.* John, can you hear me? Wake up. Please, wake up."

Her fingers shook as she checked for a pulse at the base of his throat. Nothing. She pressed more firmly, and yes, there it was. Faint but steady.

His tan skin was pale. Perspiration covered his face and chest. She checked to see if he was breathing.

Barely, his breath coming in such soft wafts, it was almost nonexistent.

Merde. She had to do something to stop this madness.

Turning her face to her captor, she whispered, "He's dead. Your man killed him!"

"He's not dead, but nice try." Black Mask bent over the man he called Mattock, gun trained on her as he went through a similar routine to check the man's pulse. Straightening, he kicked the guy's leg. "Worthless SOB. He *is* dead."

Lucie shifted as much as she could to shield John. Leaning her face close to his, she placed a hand on his lower abdomen, the other on his chest, pretending to cry. Softly, she whispered in his ear. "Hang in there. I'm going to take care of this. Everything will be okay."

Accepting her assessment of John, Black Mask sat and scanned the laptop's screen. He gave her a glance, laid the gun near the keyboard, and started typing. "Try anything and I'll shoot Quick, understand?"

Oh, she understood. Tears leaked out her eyes and she sniffled. "How do you know his name?"

He snorted, removed his mask and a translucent looking patch from his Adam's apple. When he looked straight at her, his eyes were hard, unemotional.

Goose flesh rose on her arms. Betrayal clawed at her. "*You.*"

"Yep, me."

Matt Saunders. The FBI agent who'd taken her statement after Dmitri's abuse and counseled her like she was his own daughter. The man who'd been welcomed in by the Morgan family because he'd made sure to keep the kidnapping out of the public eye, and had seemed to truly care about Lucie and Zara.

Now he'd replaced Dmitri in Lucie's ongoing nightmare. "Why? Why are you doing this?"

Returning to his typing, he ignored her question. "Unlike Quick to hook up with a woman for more than a single night. He's a player, you know. I read his profile. Never hangs around 'til dawn. I was counting on him to be long gone before midnight tonight. He must want your money as badly as I do."

The bastard! Her attention scanned the kitchen. Plenty of weapons here, but how could she get to one without him killing John? "He doesn't care about my money."

"Doesn't he? He's got a hero complex. Save the day and all

that. Believe me, sweetheart, that only carries you so far in life. I should know. The Bureau never appreciated me." Past tense.

She could almost hear John's voice. *Buy time. Keep him talking.* "You're no longer with the FBI?"

"The Bureau and I had a falling out. I left."

"So now you're a criminal?"

"I was always a criminal. That's what made me so attractive to them. Honestly, I only wanted to take care of my mother. That's how it started. I got inside the heads of the crappy deviants the FBI hunted, and knew how to fight them with my hacking skills. After a while, being the good guy got boring, and it sure as hell didn't pay enough. I instituted a couple of enterprises on the side using the Bureau's resources. Worked like magic until I sold your family's information to Dmitri. That's what started the whole thing. Too bad Pegasus put an end to him before I got my final payoff."

Lucie's nails dug into her palms so hard, she felt the skin slice. "Your mother must be so proud."

He raised a finger. "Don't you talk about my mother."

He knew all about her family, but it seemed his was the catalyst for this. Lucie wanted to call the poor woman every name in the book just to get back at him. Instead, she feigned interest. "What happened to her?"

Saunders sat back, crossed his arms. "Your father. He stole her money, what little she had. She couldn't pay for the cancer drugs she needed. Couldn't pay for the treatments. Someone started snooping around my side enterprises and I had to put them to bed. I couldn't help her make the house or car payments. She died with nothing." He leaned forward and sneered. "All because of Charles Morgan."

"My father never stole a dime from anyone."

The laptop beeped. He watched something on the screen, eyes narrowing. "And we're in."

In to what? Her bank account?

The clock on the wall read eleven fifty-seven. Once he got the money, would he kill her and John?

Yes. She'd seen his face, knew who he was. While he wasn't wielding a needle with a biological nightmare in it like Dmitri had, he was no better.

Tap, tap, tap. "After my dad died a few years ago, my mother put his insurance money into a fund. A fund Charles Morgan Investment Services recommended. The damn thing tanked last year. She couldn't work because of the cancer and she never had health insurance. When she went to get her money, there was less than a thousand dollars left. By the time they took out taxes and fees, she got jack squat."

Jack squat. An unfamiliar term but the meaning was clear. "I'm sorry, but my father did not kill her. There are no guarantees with investments."

Saunders's face hardened. "Spouting the company line? You rich bastards are all the same. You think you're above the rest of us."

Another beep.

He smiled. "Midnight."

Picking up the gun, he motioned her to the table.

Reluctantly, she rose and made her way to the chair he vacated. The gun found its way to her temple. On the screen, a prompt asked for her name and the password needed to access her account.

"Put in your password."

"Couldn't you hack my account?"

"I don't want to leave a trace, and erasing my digital fingerprints would take too much time."

Time. She and John were running out of the precious stuff.

"Besides," he continued, using the end of the gun to move

her hair away from her neck. "We'd miss this quality time together. Now type the password."

"I don't remember it."

He jammed the gun into her temple. "Put in the damn password. Now."

"This is a new account set up specifically for the fund. The password is something like sixteen characters long and was sent to me by my father's attorney. I didn't memorize it."

"You've got to be kidding."

She was, but the lie might work.

He studied her for a second. Turned the gun on John.

"Search your memory harder, then. Otherwise, I'll shoot him in the head."

The risk was too great that he would do it. She raised a hand and pecked a couple of keys, pretending she couldn't remember all the characters.

"Hurry the fuck up."

"I'm trying. Give me a minute."

The gun went off without warning, the blast echoing in her ears. She recoiled. "John!"

He hadn't moved and there was no wound on his head from a bullet. On his chest lay wood splinters from the overhead beam where the shot had torn through cedar.

"You have thirty seconds," Saunders ground out, once more pointing the gun at John.

Lucie swallowed and scooted back up to the laptop. Her fingers were shaking so bad, she could barely hit the correct keys.

But she did. All sixteen of them.

The moment the bank accepted the password, Saunders shoved her out of the chair to the floor, making himself at home.

Lucie hated giving in so easily but was relieved he'd moved the gun off John. She crawled across the floor and knelt beside him once more. "John? Can you hear me?" she whispered, searching for a pulse in his wrist.

It was so faint, she hung on, using her other hand to stroke his face and brush a lock of hair from his forehead. He was burning up and clammy at the same time. "I'm so sorry."

Behind her, Saunders was typing, pausing, typing some more. "Gotcha."

If ever there was time to find a weapon, this was it. He was too distracted by her money to pay attention to her.

Lucie looked over her shoulder at the kitchen sink, the broken glasses on the floor. A knife? A piece of glass? Neither of those would be worth much against a gun.

A flash of silver near the island caught her eye. The cake server. She released John's hand and stretched out a leg. If she could extend her foot a few more inches, she might be able to get it...

A pressure on her hand stopped her. John's hand wrapped around her wrist. His eyes were still closed, his breathing shallow, but something had changed.

He was awake. Alive and lucid, by the force of his grip.

The scrape of chair legs warned her Saunders was getting up. Lucie braced, waiting for him to yank her hair or shoot her in the back.

"Time to go, Lucie," he sing-songed, his ugly presence looming behind her. His voice was light. Proud, even.

There was no way she was going anywhere with him. She stared at John, willing him to know that she loved him. That her last view was of him. "You have my money. Leave and I won't tell the FBI or the police that it was you. If you're as good as you say you are they'll never catch you."

"True. But I can't take the chance that you'll grow a pair and tell them anyway." He shoved the laptop in a backpack and hoisted it onto his shoulders. "So you and I have to take a little

trip outside. The blizzard's over and I have transportation waiting. You're coming with me until I'm out of the country. Call it
a security precaution. A good hacker always covers his tracks."

Lucie was about to tell him to go to hell when the jerk to
her hair finally came, hauling her to her feet. Her wrist broke
free of John's hand, but he didn't move. Didn't open his eyes.

"Move," Saunders demanded.

He tossed a coat at her, once again aiming the gun at John's
head. She obeyed, her mind racing for some way to end this.
No way was she leaving John's side.

"You'll need boots."

Boots. Her boots has super thick soles and some righteous
heels. Good for pummeling a bad guy, and maybe leading him
away from the kitchen would give John the chance to do something. If he stayed conscious. "They're in the living room."

He waved the end of the gun at her. She led the way. She
sat on the bench under the security system and tugged on one,
then the other. Saunders opened the door and stood looking out
at the snowy lake, tinged blue in the dark. Biting cold air
snaked inside and wrapped around Lucie's legs. She kept one
eye on the kitchen doorway. No John.

Standing, she decided this was her best chance. Saunders's
back was to her. She could jump him from behind and...

John appeared, face set in grim determination and a gun in
hand. He aimed it at Saunders, hand trembling, and pulled the
trigger.

Lucie flinched, but there was no loud bang, only a soft
click.

No bullet. John's brows slammed together and he pulled
again.

Click.

Lucie's heart slammed hard against her ribs. Either the gun
was out of bullets or it had misfired.

Saunders whirled, eyes going wide as he saw the gun. His own came up, but John tossed his weapon aside, rushing by her to tackle him.

The impact sent both men out the door, Saunders's gun firing uselessly into the air. Together they plunged into the snow.

They rolled once, twice, three times. John, in nothing but sweatpants, was quickly covered with snow. Saunders's gun went flying, disappearing into a snowbank, as he landed with his back against the ATV sitting on the edge of the lake. John head-butted Saunders, smacking him backward into one of the wheels.

The hit stunned him briefly, and Lucie dashed out onto the lawn to look for the gun. Scrambling through the snow, she heard the sound of muffled fighting, shouting, and grunting. A quick glance back showed both men trying to rise to their feet and gain the upper hand.

She did the opposite, dropping to her knees and sweeping snow away from the spot where she thought the gun had landed. Nothing. She dug harder, and as she glanced over at the fight, she saw Saunders land a punch in John's injured side.

John went down, and Lucie's heart exploded with anger. Leaping to her feet, she slipped and nearly fell, cartwheeling her arms to keep her balance. John kicked out and caught Saunders in the thigh, sending him stumbling around the end of the ATV. The backpack fell from his shoulders and Lucie dove after it. One good swing to Saunders's head and the laptop he so prized would be the very thing to bring him down.

She stretched toward the backpack. John sprang up, glanced at her, then at Saunders. The man was climbing up onto the ATV. The engine roared to life, tires digging in and pulling away.

With a loud, ear-piercing yell, John plowed forward and

leaped on him. The ATV skidded sideways off the incline onto the lake. Two wheels left the ground, spinning for a second in midair before John's weight took Saunders over the side.

The cart attached to the ATV broke loose as both men and the ATV hit the lake and spun in circles. Saunders and John skated on their backs to a stop while the ATV righted itself, and the tires dug in again.

Lucie gasped. The ATV was headed right for them. Either it was an older model with no kill switch or the switch had been disabled.

John rolled, grabbing Saunders by the hood of his coat and jerking him into the ATV's path. The impact made a deafening crunch. Lucie flinched, covering her ears. The cart skidded past John and crashed into the ATV, now stalled on top of Saunders.

Several seconds passed, the only sound the ATV's motor. Lucie's breath came fast, her pulse pounding loudly in her ears. She struggled to her feet. "John!"

He came up on all fours, lifting a hand in a *stop* signal. "Stay there."

"You're hurt, and you're barely dressed. We need to—"

"Stay. There!"

She pulled up short, watching him as he crawled over to Saunders's body and checked for a pulse. He sat back on his ankles after a several gut-wrenching seconds, exhaustion oozing from every pore. "He's dead, Lucie," he called. "It's over."

Ignoring his demand to stay where she was, she rushed the ice, falling down next to him and hugging him to her. She laughed with relief and tried not to cry. Failed.

His hand stroked her hair like she was child. His voice came out soft and low. "You did good, darlin', but I need you to do one more thing for me, okay?"

She lifted her head and nodded through the tears.

"There's a helicopter on its way, but I won't be awake when

it lands. Tell them I've been knifed in the back, could be my kidney, and I need..."

His eyelids fluttered closed. He sank sideways, one hand fumbling in his pants pocket. Two cell phones fell out. Hers and his.

She shook his shoulders, slapped his cheeks. Tried to get him upright again. "John, wake up. What do you need?"

He didn't respond, his body totally limp.

For the first time ever, French failed her. English did not. "God*damn* it! Don't you do this to me." She had to get him inside and warm him up. She tugged at his dead weight. "I love you, John! Do you hear me? I love you and I need you."

He moaned, opened his eyes. Relief swamped through her. With some effort, the two of them leveraged him into a sitting position. "I can't feel my feet," he murmured. "Grab my boots and coat."

In the distance, she heard a *womp*ing noise.

The helicopter.

"I'll be right back," she promised, picking up both phones and running for the cabin.

The phones rang, one after the other. The display on John's showed a weird number, but she'd seen it before on Zara's phone.

Langley. The CIA.

Lucie's phone ID read Zara's number.

Brushing tears off her face, she answered her phone as she made it to the cabin's front door. "John's in trouble."

"I know," her sister answered. "Help's on the way. Are you okay?"

No. "What should I do?"

"Unlock the front door and let the men in the helicopter inside. They can help him."

No need to unlock the door. "He's bleeding. He said it was his kidney."

A pause. Zara spoke with her hand over the phone.

Probably to Lawson.

Lucie located John's boots and coat, headed back out. Her pulse jumped when she saw John was now stood. Lucie smiled.

In the background, she heard Lawson swear on Zara's end.

"Luce?" Zara came back on the phone. "Lawson said he's going to need emergency surgery. They'll take him directly to the medical center. We'll come get you and take you there."

John's phone quit ringing and started again. The noise of the helicopter blades echoed over the lake. Lucie raised her voice to Zara. "I'm going with him."

She disconnected before her sister could try to dissuade her. Picked up John's phone and answered it.

"Who is this?" a male voice demanded.

"Lucie Morgan. Who are you?"

"Conrad Flynn. Might remember me from your last stint in Europe."

She didn't. His name, yes. He was director of the spy group and Zara's boss, but the only person she *really* remembered from her so-called *stint* was John. Everyone else was a blur. "Before you tell me I can't go with John on that helicopter, let's get one thing straight. I'm calling the shots here, not you."

Silence. Then, "How bad is he?"

"He's hurt..." Her voice wobbled, but she smiled as John started toward her. "I'm not sure how badly."

Across the expanse, John's walk was more of a shuffle, and he was holding his side, but the fact he was walking was a good sign, right?

Flynn sighed on the other end. "He's one tough SOB, so don't give up on him."

She would never give up on him. "He saved my life. Again."

John raised a hand, reaching for her as he drew closer to the edge of the lake where the ATV had hit. "I have to go, Director."

"Keep this phone on you. I'll call you again in fifteen minutes."

The line went dead.

Lucie shoved the phone into her pocket and started forward.

CRACK!

John froze, looked down, then up at Lucie, his eyes wide. "Stay there!"

Panic grabbed her by the throat. *No.* "John! Don't move!" The ice...the lake...it had to be frozen solid. Why was it cracking? "Don't—"

Another crack echoed across the lake, and *whoosh*.

Just like that, John was gone.

ELEVEN

ONE SECOND, John was hobbling toward her, the next, he was gone.

She dropped the boots and ran, screaming his name. Water rose from the jagged hole where he'd disappeared and a large crack jutted east, like a finger pointing at her.

She yelled his name again and his head bobbed to the surface. One arm flung out and he grabbed onto an icy mound of snow, spewing water and gasping. Lucie flopped onto her stomach, shimmied forward opposite the crack, and reached out with both hands.

His other arm emerged and he clutched her forearm. Locking both hands on him, she tugged, digging her toes and knees into the snow and scooting backward as she heaved.

He was too heavy. She tugged again, gritting her teeth.

His teeth chattered so hard, she could barely understand him when he yelled over the sound of the approaching helicopter. "Careful. Ice...may...break...again."

"I won't let you fall!"

He met her eyes. There was admiration there. Even a little awe.

Overhead, the helicopter appeared from behind a grove of aspen trees, its noisy blades kicking up snow and blinding her. John used the mound of snow and her counterweight to heave his upper body out of the water, but that seemed to tax the last of his energy. He flopped facedown onto the ice.

Tremors shook his body and Lucie was afraid he'd slip back in. She was shaking, too, her body numb with the wintry cold and numbing fear. Still, she dug in her toes and held on tight.

The helicopter landed on the boat dock and three men spilled out, one of them zipping up a bright orange suit. Another, dressed in military attire, stomach-crawled to her, wrapping strong hands around her ankles once he made contact. The third man stood near the dock, securing one end of a yellow harness around a beam.

The man in the orange suit carried the harness to the edge of the hole on the west side and jumped in. He bobbed in the water, locked the harness around John's torso, and after making sure everything was secure, touched the top of his head.

A signal to the man at the dock. He pulled, and at the same time, the man in the hole lifted John from the water.

Lucie's relief was so great, she laughed out loud. The sound was eaten by the blades of the rescue helo. She was so cold, the laugh sounded like a squeak in her own ears. Black dots danced again at the edges of her vision.

A second later, she was lifted and carried to the helicopter. The men loaded John onto a gurney. She accepted a blanket and watched them hoist John in beside her.

The second the door slid shut, the helicopter lifted off. John's eyes were closed and his face was ashen. What was it that he needed for her to tell these men? He'd never answered her after he took out Saunders.

She grasped his frigid, stiff hand and leaned in as the men began administering medical treatment. She needed to move out of the way, but not before she said in his ear. "Remember what you told me when you rescued me from Dmitri? 'Never give up. Never surrender.' Don't give up, now, John. Don't *ever* give up."

His hand gave hers a tiny squeeze.

TWELVE

WHAT JOHN NEEDED WAS three hours of surgery.

Once he was in the operating room, CJ, one of the rescuers, insisted Lucie see a doctor as well.

Her neck was bruised and so was her back. The doctors stuck her in a bed, put her on an IV, and ran a few tests. She felt they were unnecessary, but at least they kept her from pacing the floor while she waited for John to get out of surgery. The doctor ordered a sedative. She refused.

An hour in, Lawson and Zara arrived, and behind them came the man named Flynn. *Director* Flynn. He shooed everyone out, including Zara, shutting the door so they could speak in private. Zara, insisting she be included, complained when he ordered her to leave. Flynn gave her one hard look with his dark, steely eyes and Zara quieted and gave Lucie's arm a squeeze before allowing Lawson to lead her from the room.

Being alone with Director Flynn made Lucie nervous.

He was John's complete opposite, brimming with a tightly controlled energy that reminded her of a panther.

Drawing up a chair, he didn't start with a dozen questions like she expected. Instead, he told her a story about John in Moscow. How he'd helped stop the Russian president from starting a nuclear war and saved Flynn's best friend on top of it.

Flynn held her gaze with his. "He's a quiet hero. One of silent warriors, like Vaughn and your sister. The country owes John a lot, and no one even realizes it besides those of us who see him in action every day."

Lucie nodded. "He's my hero, too."

Over the next twenty minutes, Flynn told her more stories about John's latest missions—not specific details, but enough information so that she understood the danger and pressure he'd been under during them—and about how hard he was on himself because they didn't turn out the way he thought they should have. Then he asked her to tell him about what had happened at the Morgan cabin.

He understood John, she realized, and it was easy to talk to him once she knew that. She told him everything she remembered—leaving out the fantasy sex, because that was TMI, as Zara would say—and answered Flynn's questions to the best of her ability.

"Saunders rode in on a four-wheeler," he told her, "and from my tech guru's analysis of that laptop, he planned to fly you to Bolivia. From there to a few other out-of-the-way spots before he landed in Switzerland. The man with him was a former police officer discharged two months ago pending an investigation into excessive force charges. Saunders had promised him a chunk of your trust fund for helping him, but our guess is he planned to leave the guy high and dry."

Director Flynn sat forward and placed his elbows on his knees. His eyes were nearly black, the panther in him resurfacing. "Del, my tech guru, will get your money back, but it may be months or even longer before the investigation is over and all the bureaucratic red tape is cut."

"I don't care about the money."

He nodded. "Your father does."

Her father. How was she going to face him? What would he say about the cabin? About the missing money? Would he blame her?

Lucie found she didn't care. "I want John to be my family now."

Another nod. A corner of his mouth twitched in what she took for a smile. "John's a lucky man."

No, he wasn't. "After this, he'll never want to see me again. All I do is cause him trouble."

Flynn waved off her statement. "The man thrives on trouble."

"Saunders had a file on John. He said he's not the type to ever settle down."

"And Saunders profiled you and your dad as *rich bastards who don't care about anyone else,* that's what you quoted him as saying, right? Is that label accurate?"

"No."

He shrugged.

Point taken. Lucie looked down at the IV in her arm. "Can you get the doctor to discharge me?"

"Shouldn't be a problem, if you're up for it." He held out a hand. "You're a lot like Zara, you know that?"

She accepted his handshake. "She's tougher. And nicer. But I hope to be like her when it comes to finding a good man who doesn't care what my last name is or how much I'm worth."

"I think you've found him."

"I think I have, too."

THIRTEEN

John woke in a recovery room with faded shades allowing slivers of sunlight to creep in around the edges. A heart monitor beeped next to an IV pole. He floated in a sweet, drug-induced haze...one where Lucie was sitting in a chair by the bed, her hand intertwined with his as she slept with her head next to his chest.

He gave her hand a squeeze, watched her waken. Her tousled head lifted, a smile like he'd never seen breaking over her face. Amazed. Hopeful. Happy.

He gave her a loopy smile in return. He couldn't feel much of his body, and his mouth was so dry his voice cracked when he spoke. "Tell me...you're...okay."

Her eyes glistened as if she might cry. "Better than okay. The doctors saved your kidney and said you'll be back to work in a few weeks. The ice bath gave you hypothermia but it also stopped you from bleeding out."

"Thank God you're alright." His memory was fuzzy. "Did I kill him?"

"Both men are dead."

He tried to call up some remorse. Failed.

She rose, leaning over him, her beautiful eyes searching his. Looking for those answers he wasn't sure he had. He hated she had witnessed such a horrible thing, especially after living through Dmitri. She'd have nightmares on top of nightmares now. "Lucie, I—"

Dipping her head, she touched his lips, a soft, sweet kiss that told him it was okay.

Even in his woozy state, her lips sent his body into over-drive. When she started to pull away, he found the strength to grab her arms and kiss her back, deepening it and hoping such a simple thing could convey all the pent up emotions he couldn't articulate.

Her lips parted and she sighed into his mouth. He took that as a good sign, enjoying the familiar feel of it. Of her.

Home.

The drugs didn't stop his lower half from responding to the heat now pouring through his body. When they broke apart, Lucie could obviously feel how aroused he was, and laughed. "You just had major surgery."

Didn't he know it. Already his side and back were waking up, burning and cramping from the rush of fresh adrenaline she'd given rise to, regardless of the drugs. "What can I say? I can't resist you."

She straightened and turned serious, the smile fading slightly. "So you'll stick around this time?"

"Does it look like I'm going anywhere?"

A knock on the door interrupted them. Charles Morgan filled the frame, commanding as always with his mere presence. "May I come in?"

Lucie tensed. "The nurses said I was the only person allowed for now."

John supposed Lucie was the closest thing he had to family

outside of Lawson, but she still wasn't a relative. "How *did* you get them to let you in?" he asked.

A flush rose on her cheeks. "I told them I was your wife."

John smiled.

Without missing a beat, she smiled back.

Home.

Charles cleared his throat and appeared chagrined. "The nurse said it was okay for me to visit for a minute or two. It's important. I need to talk to both of you."

Lucie shifted her body, shielding John and his roaring erection. "Now is not the time to talk about money."

Ignoring the pain in his back, John stretched to peer around her.

Charles stepped into the room, his gaze roaming over Lucie as if he were seeing her for the first time. "I don't care about the money, Lucie."

"You don't?"

"My daughter was kidnapped and nearly killed. *Again.*" He moved forward. Stopped. "Right now, I'm after some revenge, which is unfortunately, out of my hands, according to the CIA, FBI, and others. Along with that, I need to apologize to someone very special." His gaze searched hers. "Lucie, honey, I'm sorry."

That seemed to knock the wind out of her. Her butt hit the side of John's bed. "For what?"

Charles put his hands in his pockets. "Every time I look at you, I see your mother. You may not believe this, but I cared for her a great deal. It's difficult for me to...ah...not think of her whenever I see you. I was giving you the money to relieve my guilt over what I did to her, not being able to marry her, and, in turn, to you. But now...I just want you to come home."

The drugs were screwing with John. He could have sworn there were tears in the man's eyes.

Charles wasn't done. He walked around the bed to John's other side. "And you, young man, I owe you a great debt."

John didn't want the man in debt to him. All he cared about was Lucie. "I love Lucie, sir, and if she'll have me, I'd like to stick around." *Permanently.*

His future plans must have shown in his eyes. Charles smiled a knowing smile. "If that's what Lucie wants, you're welcome in our home, anytime. I've been an idiot and I hope you won't hold that against me, son."

Son. John's head rejected the term like always, but his heart didn't. He squeezed Lucie's hand again. "Lucie's my home, sir. I know that now. Wherever she is, I'll be there."

John felt her reassuring squeeze back.

"Very good." Charles glanced from John to Lucy. "Olivia and I have discussed it. I'm selling that damn cabin and Olivia wants to find a weekend place closer to Arlington. Closer to you and Zara, before the baby comes. What do you think, Lucie? Can you stand having us around a bit more?"

Lucie leaned across the bed and threw her arms around Charles, nearly making the man fall on top of John. She was so full of life, so full of everything he'd always needed and never had. He wanted to grab her and hug her to him and never let her go.

Charles gave his daughter an awkward pat on the back, and glanced at John with that awkward male look, as though emotional displays were true suffering. "I believe my minute is up. I'll let the others know you're all right."

"The others?" Lucie asked.

"The rest of the family. They've been calling and stopping by. Everyone's quite worried about both of you."

Lucie made a surprised sound in the back of her throat. "*Vraiment?*"

"Yes, really."

She walked her father to the door, hugged him again, and saw him out. Once he was gone, she came back and sat by the bed. "I have a family. A real family."

"Looks that way."

"Not them." She met his eyes. "You."

The pain in his back meant nothing when she looked at him that way. His past failures had less hold. "I've never said this to anyone before, Luce, but I, ah…"

He took a deep breath to steady his shaking body. To steady his heart. "I love you."

"Good thing, since you're going to be at my mercy for a few weeks."

The sheet tented again. "I hope to be at your mercy for the rest of my life."

She stood and leaned over him, touching his lips with hers. "I love you, John Quick."

He kissed her back. "We still on for Disneyland?"

"*Bien sûr.*" This time, she laughed, light and easy. "The happiest place on earth, *oui?*"

"*Oui,*" he answered, knowing the happiest place on earth for him would always be with her.

ACKNOWLEDGMENTS

John and Lucie have had a long journey to their happily ever after, and it never would have happened if not for the dedicated readers of the Super Agent series, who kept asking for it. Thank you, readers.

As always, I'm indebted to my fellow authors and those covert sources who agreed to talk to me. When I sent out a call for help, author Laurie London put me in touch with white hat guru, Jaye, who walked me through the ins and outs of hacking. Scary, but fascinating.

For a suspense author, there's nothing like having a few FBI insiders as part of your family and friends plan, and I appreciate the ones who gave me the idea for the perfect bad guy to pit against John.

ROMANTIC SUSPENSE & MYSTERIES BY MISTY EVANS

SEALS of Shadow Force Series: Spy Division

Man Hunt

Man Killer

Man Down

SEALs of Shadow Force Series

Fatal Truth

Fatal Honor

Fatal Courage

Fatal Love

Fatal Vision

Fatal Thrill

Risk

The SCVC Taskforce Series

Deadly Pursuit

Deadly Deception

Deadly Force

Deadly Intent

Deadly Affair, A SCVC Taskforce novella

Deadly Attraction

Deadly Secrets

Deadly Holiday, A SCVC Taskforce novella

Deadly Target

Deadly Rescue

Deadly Bounty

The Super Agent Series

Operation Sheba

Operation Paris

Operation Proof of Life

Operation Lost Princess

Operation Ambush

Operation Sleeping With the Enemy

The Justice Team Series (with Adrienne Giordano)

Stealing Justice

Cheating Justice

Holiday Justice

Exposing Justice

Undercover Justice

Protecting Justice

PNR & UF BY MISTY/NYX

Paranormal Romance

Witches Anonymous Step 1

Jingle Hells, Witches Anonymous Step 2

Wicked Souls, Witches Anonymous Step 3

Dark Moon Lilith, Witches Anonymous Step 4

Dancing With the Devil, Witches Anonymous Step 5

Devil's Due, Witches Anonymous Step 6

Dirty Deeds, Witches Anonymous Step 7

Wicked Wedding, Witches Anonymous Step 8

Urban Fantasy

Revenge Is Sweet, Kali Sweet Urban Fantasy Series, Book 1

Sweet Chaos, Kali Sweet Urban Fantasy Series, Book 2

Sweet Soldier, Kali Sweet Urban Fantasy Series, Book 3

Sweet Curse, Kali Sweet Urban Fantasy Series, Book 4

Paranormal Romantic Suspense

Soul Survivor, Moon Water Series, Book 1

Soul Protector, Moon Water Series, Book 2

Cozy Mysteries (writing as Nyx Halliwell)

Sister Witches Of Raven Falls Mystery Series

Of Potions and Portents

Of Curses and Charms

Of Stars and Spells

Of Spirits and Superstition

Confessions of a Closet Medium Cozy Mystery Series

(Coming 2020)

Pumpkins & Poltergeists

Once Upon a Witch Cozy Mystery Series

(Coming 2020)

Psychic Sisters Cozy Mystery Series

(Coming 2021)

ABOUT THE AUTHOR

USA TODAY Bestselling Author Misty Evans has published more than sixty novels and writes romantic suspense, urban fantasy, and paranormal romance. Under her pen name, Nyx Halliwell, she also writes cozy mysteries.

She got her start writing in 4th grade when she won second place in a school writing contest with an essay about her dad. Since then, she's written nonfiction magazine articles, started her own coaching business, become a yoga teacher, and raised twin boys on top of enjoying her fiction career.

When not reading or writing, she enjoys music, movies, and hanging out with her husband, twin sons, and three spoiled puppies. A registered yoga teacher and Master Reiki Practitioner, she shares her love of chakra yoga and energy healing, but still hasn't mastered levitating.

Get free reads, all the latest news, and alerts about sales when you sign up for her newsletter at www.readmistyevans.com. To find out more about her holistic healing practice, please visit www.crystalswithmisty.com.

LETTER FROM MISTY

Hello Beautiful Reader!

Thank you for reading this story! It is an honor and a privilege to write stories for you.

I hope you enjoyed this book, and I'd like to ask a favor – would you mind leaving a review at your favorite retailer? I'd really appreciate it, and reviews help other readers find books they will love too.

If you'd like to learn about my other books, sales, and special promotions, please sign up for my newsletter at www.readmistyevans.com.

Grab special edition box sets and get new releases before they come out at retailers by visiting my direct buy website www.mistyevansbooks.com. I have sales and offer NEW RELEASES early and at a discount!! Check it out.

I also have a holistic business, Crystals With Misty, and invite you to check out my website www.crystalswithmisty.com for information on my services.

Last but not least, if you enjoy clean, cozy mysteries, visit my pen name www.nyxhalliwell.com to see those books!

Thank you and happy reading!

Misty